HAZARD IN THE HOROSCOPE

KARI LEE TOWNSEND

PUBLISHER'S NOTE: This is a work of fiction. Names, characters, places, and incidents either are the product of the author's imagination or are used fictitiously. Any resemblance to actual persons, living or dead, business establishments, events, or locales is entirely coincidental.

Published by Oliver Heber Books

OLIVER
HEBER
BOOKS

Published by Oliver-Heber Books

0 9 8 7 6 5 4 3 2 1

"You don't have to do this, Granny," I said to my grandmother, Gertrude, after I finished unloading her belongings from my yellow VW Bug with flowers painted on the sides.

I carried her things into Divine Inspiration Inn, the quaint little bed and breakfast on the outskirts of our small, upstate New York town. Snow was softly falling, blanketing the ground in a carpet of white fluff. The air was still, and everything was calm and peaceful. It was actually quite serene and idyllic.

Granny Gert had first moved in with me a few months after I'd arrived in Divinity. Having lived in New York City with my parents my entire life, I had never been on my own. Considering I had been twenty-nine at that point in my life, I'd figured it was about time I grew up and left the proverbial nest, except everyone thought I needed help.

In more ways than one.

"Oh, pish posh." Granny waved her wrinkled, dark-spotted hand at me, her snappy brown eyes sparkling devilishly. "Your mother needs me more than you do now, and I didn't imagine I would ever hear myself say that about such a strong, independent woman like her. Besides, you and your new *fiancé* need some alone time."

Granny tightened her plastic rain cap over her fabulous snow-white head of hair, even though there wasn't a cloud in sight. It had turned white at the tender age of sixteen from a battle with scarlet fever, but she'd never colored it. Admittedly, her hair was the envy of all the elderly ladies in town. Granny wasn't taking a chance on messing up her pride and joy.

She adjusted her winter coat over her ancient apron made out of old flour sacks. Having lived through the depression, my granny was all about waste not want not. After Grandpa Frank's passing, she had more money than she knew what to do with, stored in freezer bags and old shoe boxes because she didn't trust the banks or the government. But even though she was rich, that didn't mean she would ever stop being frugal.

My parents, Donald and Vivian Meadows, were high society, with careers as a world-renowned heart surgeon and an esteemed lawyer. They'd named me Sylvia in high hopes I would follow in one of their footsteps, and they couldn't seem to accept my choice of fortune-telling as a profession. Not to mention they had a hard time believing in my psychic ability, no matter how many inexplicable signs they were faced with. They still hadn't gotten over the fact that their only child had changed her name to Sunshine—or Sunny for short.

"Must be nice to feel needed," I said with a sigh, adjusting my heavily fringed sweater shawl over my turtleneck and long flowy skirt.

I had always been close to my father, even though he didn't really understand me any more than my mother did, but my mother had never really been close to me at all. In fact, she'd taken more of a shine to my best friend, Joanne Burnham—now Joanne West since she'd recently married the love of her life, Carpenter Cole, in September. Even Jo's cousin, Zoe, who had come to town to help plan Jo's wedding, seemed to have more in common with my mother than I did. I always felt like an afterthought. I'd moved to Divinity to break away from that world and start fresh. Of course, trouble had followed me in the form of four murders, which brought out the overbearing protective instincts of my parents more than ever.

"I can see the wheels in that sharp mind of yours turning something fierce." Granny winked. "Quit fretting so much, sweetie. Your mother loves you more than *she* even knows. She simply has a hard time showing it. Maybe now that she's retired, she'll soften up a bit. She didn't move to Divinity only to take over running the inn, you know."

"Oh, trust me, I know. They both think they need to take care of me still. I'm a grown woman, engaged to a detective. I think I can manage just fine on my own."

"Mitch is a wonderful man, and we are all thrilled with the idea of having him as part of the family. They're not worried about you, Sunny. They want to be a part of your life, especially with the thought of grandchildren running around."

My stomach flipped, and the acid that was becoming a regular occurrence churned up my esophagus. Jo, who was pregnant with twins and due in three months, had said pretty much the same thing to me recently. The problem was I didn't even know if I wanted children, which worried me because I'd never really discussed that with Mitch. And *that* was the main reason I hadn't picked a date for our wedding yet.

What if he wanted children and I didn't? Or vice versa. Would that be a deal breaker? The stress was killing me, and Mitch was growing impatient with my waffling. I owed him an explanation for my fears, but we'd been getting along so well I didn't want to do anything to jeopardize our peaceful truce.

"You look pale. Did I say something to upset you?" Granny stared at me with a concerned expression.

I pasted a smile on my face. "I'm fine. Just a little indigestion from lunch." I rubbed my aching stomach.

"Or the thought of seeing your parents again so soon," Granny said knowingly. "No worries, sugarplum. I'll keep them out of your business. That's another reason I decided to move in with them. Not only do they need help to run this place, but now you have eyes and ears on the inside." She twittered conspiratorially.

After the innkeeper had died during Jo's wedding reception, my mother had been the number one suspect. Then after her name was finally cleared, she'd gone back to the Big Apple. I'd been relieved, but that had been short-lived. She'd informed me that the incident had put her life in perspective. She'd taken a step back and realized it was time to leave the stressful world of law.

My father had taken a bit longer to agree to leave the rewarding life as a cardiologist, but he too had come to know when it was time to slow down and enjoy the little things. Especially now that I was engaged, which was something neither of them had ever thought possible. Besides, my father adored my mother, and if she wanted the inn, then that was what she would have.

I was all for them retiring. Becoming my neighbors... not so much.

"Have I told you how much I love you lately?" I hugged my granny hard. We were so much alike in many ways. Yet another thing that drove my mother crazy.

"Oh, twiddle dee dee you're going to make me all misty." Granny patted my back. "I love you too, Sunny. Now, you take care of my boy Morty. I expect to see fresh bowties on him every week. Don't let him fool you. He likes them as much as I like making them. I'm gonna miss that ornery kitty." Granny had taken to making bowties from all the old curtains that had come with my house when I moved in.

The problem was, Granny didn't sew nearly as well as she baked.

"You've got it," I responded, knowing Morty wasn't going to like that one bit. "You can see him anytime, you know. It's not like you're moving out of town."

"Good girl, I knew I could count on you to keep my main squeeze looking dapper. And I'm sure I will see my little fella plenty."

Granny had taken a shine to Morty and couldn't help dressing him up like Grandpa Frank. Morty didn't like many people, but he'd bonded with Granny in a special way. He seemed to sense she needed him, and he loved the attention, though he'd never let you know it. I wouldn't mind letting Granny take him to keep her happy, even though I would miss him something fierce. The problem was, he would never leave me. We were kindred spirits, and together for better or worse in this crazy ride called life. The only trouble was that he and *my* main squeeze Mitch didn't like each other much.

"Now fetch my pumpkin cookie jar from the back

seat, please," Granny went on. "I can't store my cookies in anything else, you know. They just don't taste the same."

"Absolutely, and you're right. Your cookies are amazing for a reason. I think Grandpa Frank added a special touch to this cookie jar when he gave it to you."

"Special touch?" She laughed. "The only thing that old geezer did was break the lid." Her smile remained, but I could still see how much she missed him shining in her eyes.

"Exactly." I gave her a mischievous smile. "The tin-foil-covered plate you put on top has to be the secret, because I've never tasted cookies as delicious as yours."

"Maybe someday I'll fill you in on the *real* secret." Her eyes twinkled with something mysterious.

"I'll hold you to that." I laughed and wondered if she was more like me than even I realized.

"Hold her to what?" my mother asked as she walked out of the inn, dressed head to toe in a gorgeous forest green suit and wool coat, her golden blond hair perfectly coifed.

I had to fight hard to stop myself from shaking my head. She looked ready to go to court rather than run a bed and breakfast, but some changes would take a lot longer to instill. She had no clue her clientele in Divinity would be vastly different from the five-star circle of people she ran around with in the Big Apple. Far be it from me to enlighten her. She wouldn't listen anyway.

It had taken a few months for my mother to settle her affairs and move to Divinity permanently. Now that it was January and she had officially retired, she was hitting the ground running with all the changes she planned to make. The inn had always been charming, but she'd constantly criticized the former owner of not taking the necessary steps to advance the inn to the next level and allow it to reach its full potential.

There was no way she would make that mistake herself. There was construction going on all over the grounds—as much as they could complete, given that it was winter. My mother wanted everything done by the spring. She simply couldn't understand that not everyone in Divinity would agree with what the *next level* should be. More like she refused to believe, as my mother was a very smart woman.

"There you are, darling," my father boomed, as he strolled out of the inn, wearing so many clothes he looked like a big puffy marshmallow man.

"Good heavens, Donald," my mother sputtered. "What on earth are you wearing this time?"

She was used to seeing him dressed smartly and only partaking in dignified activities appropriate for people such as themselves who ran in a certain prestigious social circle. She definitely couldn't seem to understand that retirement meant two very different things to each of them. My father stared back at her with a beaming expression on his handsome face, his steel gray Ken-doll hair covered with a fuzzy hat with floppy side panels that draped over his ears.

"Harry says ice fishing reels in the bigger fish, and men who ice fish are of a hardy breed." He slapped his chest. "That's me."

"Hardy breed you say? Is that what you are?" my mother asked with an innocent expression and tone, but I could see her struggle not to roll her eyes.

"That's right, Viv. I'm a retired man now. No more stress of saving lives or trying to impress everyone or trying to live up to the whole world's opinion of me. I feel free doing whatever the hell I want for a change, and just living a life of ease."

My mother gasped, and this time my father fought not to roll *his* eyes.

"Look at Harry," he went on. "He used to control the fate of people's lives in a courtroom, and he is happier than I've ever seen him now that he's retired. You were right. This was a great idea."

"Harry is old enough to be your father."

"Even better. He's had plenty more years to discover the secret to life and happiness and retirement. You should talk to Fiona, or your mother, for that matter."

My mother harrumphed and stood a bit straighter. "I don't need anyone, and neither should you. Running the inn was a great idea. You, bumbling around like the abominable snowman, pretending to be something you're not is *not* a great idea. I can't run this inn alone, Donald."

"Then don't." My father patted her arm but held his ground, impressing me. Usually, my mother got her way in pretty much everything. "Maybe it's time you let your mother and daughter and Fiona help, Viv. You can't control everything, you know. Maybe it's time you stopped trying." He kissed her cheek, then faced me and gave me the biggest bear hug he'd ever given. It made me feel all warm inside. I liked the new Donald. My mother, not so much. "Gotta run, ladies. The fish are biting."

"But you have no clue what you're doing," my mother pointed out. "And there's barely any ice out there. Mark my words. You'll fall through and break your neck before the sun sets. You'll see I'm right."

"Harry says you need an adventurous spirit," my father went on, ignoring her negative comments and doubt. "You also need a sled to drag your gear and something warm to drink. I've got all that covered already down by the lake, and if the ice isn't safe, we'll fish from the shore." He shrugged, looking happier than I'd seen him in a long time.

My mother crossed her arms and shook her head.

"Harry also says you need a wicking layer close to the body—like shirts, pants, socks. A layer for heat—like wool, fleece, or polartech. Something for the face —like a facemask, long scarf, or neck warmer. And a final layer of a one-piece thinsulate or insulated coveralls or a goose down layer for wind breakage and warmth." He counted off his checklist on his hand as if reading from a textbook as he spoke, sporting an excited grin with every word. "I'm all set, Viv. You'll see when I come back with dinner from the lake out back. Or better yet, maybe we'll hit up the river downstream."

"Harry says, Harry says, Harry says." My mother threw up her hands. "You've gone crazy," she murmured.

"And loving every minute of it." My father waved to us all and walked away, whistling a lively tune that made me giggle and earned me a scowl from my mother.

I pressed my lips together to swallow any more laughter as I looked away.

Harry was a former judge my mother had worked with in the past. He was also Fiona Atwater's—Granny Gert's former best friend, turned enemy, turned best friend—on again, off again, on again husband. It was exhausting just thinking about the world I lived in, but I had to admit it certainly was entertaining.

"What on earth am I supposed to do with that?" my mother asked, staring after my father, at a loss for words. I wanted to say *lighten up and join him*, but she actually looked a little worried, so I didn't say anything.

Granny gazed off in the distance with a fond expression on her face that made me think of Grandpa Frank and how short life really was. "Love every minute with him," she responded to my mother softly, "because before you know it, he could be gone."

———————

"ALONE AT LAST," I SAID, AS I SAT ON MY LIVING ROOM couch in my ancient Victorian house beside Detective Mitch Stone, the love of *my* life.

A roaring fire he'd built in the fireplace crackled and popped, its yellow, red, and orange flames burning bright as he answered with, "Not entirely."

A sound like hissing laughter whispered through the room, putting Mitch on edge once more. I frowned, sending out a silent mental scolding to Morty. Knowing my big, white, immortal cat, he would get my meaning loud and clear. Just as I expected, the noise faded away. I snuggled into my big, dark, and brooding fiancé's arms, throwing my yoga pant-clad legs over his NYPD sweatpants. Lifting my face, I stared up into his. He was so rugged and sexy, with jet black curls, gray eyes, an olive complexion, and a five o'clock shadow that covered a jagged scar along his jaw. His slightly crooked nose only added to his appeal.

"I love you," I said, in barely more than a whisper.

His entire face softened, and his lips tipped up ever so slightly at the corners before he pressed them to mine. The same thrill as always zipped through me every time he touched me. "I love you, too, Tink."

He'd called me Tink, short for Tinkerbell, ever since he'd first met me. I couldn't really blame him since I called him Grumpy Pants. He thought I was too little bitty to protect myself, and I thought he was grumpier than Captain Hook. But hey, it worked for us.

I rested my head on his shoulder and he leaned his down on top of mine. It felt so right being with him, I never wanted it to end. "I can't believe it's January, and I'm thirty, and I've lived here for a year."

"And I can't believe you still haven't set a date for our wedding." His voice was a deep sexy rumble, but the underlying note of concern came through.

I winced and pulled back to look up at him. "It's not because I don't want to marry you. Please tell me you know that."

"Don't worry." He tightened his arms around me on a weary sigh. "I get it, because I know *you*. You're going to study our horoscopes and the charts and astrology and God knows what else before you find the perfect month, day—hell, *hour*—for us to get married. I would elope today if you said yes," I opened my mouth to speak until he held up his hand and continued, "but I want to make you happy."

My heart melted with love for this man. "I want to make you happy, too." I wanted to tell him about my fears over having a baby, but I was terrified. It was silly. I knew I could talk to him about anything, yet some part deep inside me froze up every time it came to this topic. "I just want everything to be perfect, and for neither of us to have any regrets. We're not getting any younger, you know."

"I'm looking forward to growing old with you. As long as I have you, I don't need anyone or anything else. I just don't like all the hoopla. I want you as my wife. End of discussion."

"You don't want anything else?" I prodded.

He looked off in the distance as though giving the matter some serious thought, and for a moment, I had hope that he would bring the subject of children up first. Of course, I couldn't get that lucky.

"A honeymoon where I can have you to myself, someplace far away would be nice," he finally said, "but other than that, I'm good." His dark eyes stared intensely at me, a hint of the curiosity and worry returning. "Why, was there something else *you* wanted?"

"I've got you. What more could I possibly want?" I smiled too wide.

He frowned suspiciously.

Morty yowled loudly, appearing from out of nowhere right above us on the couch, and we both jumped apart.

"A honeymoon it is," I blurted, then narrowed my eyes at Morty. "*Alone.*"

"Ground rules," Mitch suddenly said firmly.

"Excuse me?"

"I've decided there is something else I want. Ground rules." He stared warily at my naughty cat. "If the three of us are going to live together peacefully, I think it's time we establish some rules."

"But he's a cat," I said, trying to be rational.

Mitch smirked at me. "You and I both know he's much more than that."

"Really?" I raised my chin a notch. "So, does this mean you're finally starting to believe I'm more than just a fortune-teller?"

His eyes widened a fraction over his slip, but then his brows drew together slightly as he replied, "Well, I, um... can I plead the Fifth?"

"Sure, as long as well, I, um... can plead the Fifth on ground rules and a wedding date." I batted my eyelashes at him.

He raised an ink-black brow. "But, that's not fair."

I shrugged. "Life's not fair, Detective. You of all people should know that." I patted his hand and stood up. "Now if you'll excuse me, I need to go study my charts."

I walked out of the room and into my office—Sunny's Sanctuary—with his heavy sigh following me every step of the way. It was a lame excuse I'd given, and I wasn't mad about him not being a true believer. After almost losing him, I didn't really care about that anymore. I'd simply needed any excuse to escape before he asked me what was really bothering me. He was a great detective and he knew me too well, but I was terrified if he knew the truth, he would want something else, all right...

Like to call off our wedding for good.

2

"There's no way I can do this," Jo said from behind the mahogany bar of her first baby, Smokey Jo's Tavern.

"Yes, you can," I said with a sympathetic smile, though I was just as terrified for her. She was showing so quickly.

"I have three months to go, Sunny." She pointed to her massive belly. "How much bigger can they possibly get?"

Jo was a tall, voluptuous woman with curves in all the right places, and her husband Cole was a giant of a man. Birthing a set of his twins had to be intimidating, but right now she didn't need to hear that. What she needed was a friend.

"Stop listening to everyone's horror stories. If having a baby was that horrible, no one would ever do it again. You're one of eight children, and you're a whole lot tougher than your mother. If she can do it, then you surely can."

"My mother wasn't married to Sasquatch."

"Your mother wasn't an Amazon Queen, either."

"That's true." Jo stood a little straighter and looked

more confident by the second. "I am pretty impressive, aren't I?"

Cole walked through the kitchen door as she said that and wrapped his arms around her from behind, cradling her belly with his palms and wearing a besotted expression of love for them all. "You're beautiful and amazing and the most incredible woman I've ever met." He kissed the side of her neck.

Jo's lips tipped up at the corners, and every inch of her turned marshmallow soft. "Flattery will get you everywhere, my darling."

"I think it already did." His eyes gentled as they locked onto hers, and he leaned down to kiss her softly on the lips.

I couldn't stop the sigh from slipping out of my mouth. They were so in love and happy and fabulous together. I suddenly realized I wanted that more than anything. I loved Mitch with all my heart, and he made me ridiculously happy. Having his baby would make my life complete. The question I struggled with was would it make his life fulfilled, or would he be reliving the nightmare of not being able to protect his younger sister? I think that was why I hadn't been able to talk to him. I'd seen into his past. I knew the horror he'd gone through. Something told me he would never risk going through anything like that again.

Not even for me.

"Earth to Sunny," Jo said, as if she'd already said it several times. "Where'd you go? You look so sad and a little afraid."

I blinked. Cole had gone back into the kitchen, and Jo's cousin Zoe—who was a softer, younger replica of Jo—stood beside her. "When did you get here?"

Zoe laughed. "Wow, you really were somewhere far away. What's up?"

"Nothing, really."

"Um, yeah, that's not happening." Jo nailed me with a knowing look as she refilled the napkins on the bar. "Spill it." Being a bartender had given her an uncanny ability to read people and know when to back off and leave them alone or when to step in and lend an ear.

"You know me so well." I sipped my hot tea, reflecting on my situation.

It was Sunday afternoon. Mitch was home fiddling around in the barn. Things had been strained since our talk. I hated that and without Granny around to fill the silence, I was at a loss as to how to fix the situation.

"My house is too quiet," I finally explained.

"That's right. Granny moved in with your parents yesterday." Zoe helped stock glasses so Jo wouldn't have to lift anything. "How's that going?"

"I have no idea," I replied. "My mother's already started remodeling. She can't sit still long enough to retire and is way too uptight to venture out of her comfort zone. Meanwhile, after my father got shot and nearly died, he is all about trying new things and living life to the fullest. Harry and Fiona moved into the inn as well. My father has taken up ice fishing with Harry. Lord knows what else is on his bucket list. Granny was right. They need her more than I do."

"Wait, they are all going to live under the same roof?" Zoe gaped.

"Yes, except I can't imagine Granny and Fiona as the cooks. The Dynamic Duo might have called a truce, friendship-wise, but they are still both way too competitive for their own good. Meanwhile, Harry and my father are two peas in a pod. Having them in charge of the grounds is fine, if you can keep them away from their bucket list for long enough to tend to anything. Thank goodness Sally Clark stayed on as housekeeper. It would have been too much house for anyone else, and Frank LaLone stayed on as the maintenance man. My father might have a green thumb, but neither he nor Harry are mechanically inclined. If you ask me, there are too many people who will try to be in charge. Something tells me there are going to be more than a few bumps in the road along the way to opening day."

"It will be interesting to watch, that's for sure," Jo said, "but I don't know about your mother needing Granny more than you do." She studied me closely. "I can see that something is bothering you, when this should be the happiest time of your life. Your business is booming, there hasn't been any trouble recently, you're engaged to a great man, and you finally have the house to yourselves. What more could you possibly want?"

"I know. I'm so lucky," I said, and then burst into tears.

Jo and Zoe rushed around the bar to flank my sides, and that only made me cry harder. When I was finally finished, I wiped my face with the napkins that had magically appeared in front of me.

"Feel better?" Jo asked with a tender smile.

"Actually, I do." I laughed.

"Are you ready to tell us what that was all about?" Zoe folded her arms across her chest, becoming more and more like Jo every day.

"I want a baby."

"That's wonderful." Zoe clapped her hands. "I just love babies."

"Me too, apparently," I said in wonder, "and I didn't even realize just how much until today."

"Wow, I didn't see that one coming?" Jo's eyebrows raised so high they disappeared beneath her hairline.

"That's what I'm afraid of." My stomach rolled over. "That Mitch won't see it coming, either."

Jo covered my hand and squeezed. "Talk to him."

"I know I have to, but it's so hard. What if he doesn't want a baby?"

"He might not," Jo said honestly. "But it *is* a discussion you need to have before getting married. Look at me." She rubbed her enormous belly. "I didn't think I wanted children, and Cole was scared to death—still is if we're being completely honest—but we've both come to accept and even cherish the little family we're making. I got lucky. It could have been so much worse if he hadn't come around. You don't want that to happen to you. Mitch is a complicated man with a past that still haunts him. You need to talk to him."

"I know, hence the fear and sadness and tears." I sipped my tea, looking for comfort wherever I could get it.

"Mitch loves you so much, Sunny." Zoe hugged me. "The way he looks at you takes my breath away. He might surprise you. Then again, he might not. You have to be prepared for that. The real question is, can you live with his answer either way?"

"That is *the* question." I laughed nervously. "Speaking of the way a man looks at a woman, how are things going with Sean?" I asked Zoe, needing to take my mind off my troubles and change the subject. And just like I knew they would, my girls backed off.

Zoe's face flushed a becoming shade of pink over just the mention of Sean's name. "Good."

Jo snorted. "Don't let her fool you. They're going great. She has that man eating out of her hand, and yes, she's still a virgin."

"I can't believe Sean's abstained for over three months now." I shook my head in awe. "That has to be a record."

"He's so sweet. He hasn't pressured me at all. In fact, I've been the one having a hard time holding back, but he keeps me strong. He knows how much it means to me, and he's trying to prove he wants more than an affair. He truly wants all of me." Zoe's face flushed even brighter.

"Awww, honey, that's so awesome." I hugged her tight. "What's next for you two? Marriage maybe?"

She shrugged. "I have no clue, but I'm excited to find out. All I know for sure is that I'm happier than I've ever been."

Zoe glanced across the bar at Sean as he was setting up all the tables, preparing for the evening crowd, and her face glowed. He seemed to be pulled in her direction from the magnetism humming between them. When he looked at her, his hands grew still and everything about him gentled. His adorable dimples sank deep, and his smile said it all. The ladies' man had finally been tamed by a single woman.

Sean O'Malley was in love.

———

LATER THAT EVENING I DECIDED TO TALK TO MITCH. Jo and Zoe's happiness had given me the courage to go after my own. I'd invited him into my workspace— Sunny's Sanctuary—now that it had been repaired after a break-in had destroyed nearly everything. It was back and better than ever. Mitch and I shared a bedroom, and we all knew the rest of the house was pretty much Morty's, but my sanctuary was my personal space.

The garage had become Mitch's. It wasn't that I couldn't go in there, but it was the one place I left for him to escape to when he needed to be alone and think. The same was true with him and my office. I conducted readings in there, and Mitch had been inside many times, but mostly it was the one place for me that was truly mine alone.

He parted the strands of crystal beads and stepped inside. I'd painted the walls a soft, pale blue and had turned on my usual New Age music to relax us both. My tropical fish tank bubbled while the fireplace popped and crackled, giving off a cozy feel. I might not be able to cook, but I had a green thumb, and enjoyed the various plants and herbs I had scattered about, giving the room life and vitality. But my favorite part of all were the constellations that covered the ceiling in a sparkling imitation of the universe, glowing when the lights were dimmed.

I chose some astrological charts and zodiac signs from my selection of fortune-telling supplies on a set of shelves in the corner, and then placed them on the ancient Victorian tea table in the center of the room. "Please, have a seat." I gestured to the chair across from me.

"Why are we in here?" he asked warily, his gaze darting about as he sat down.

"I wanted to talk to you."

"You sound serious." He looked worried.

"This is a serious conversation."

He reached out and took my hands in his own. "I'm sorry."

My forehead wrinkled. "What on earth for?"

"For whatever I did wrong." He looked so helpless and admittedly adorable, reminding me of just how much I loved him.

I was already shaking my head. "You didn't do anything wrong, Mitch. I'm the one who's sorry."

His face puckered, looking confused. "Okay."

"I know I've been acting strange lately, and you have every right to want to pick a wedding date," I went on. "It's been almost four months since I asked you to marry me."

He arched a thick black brow. "I'm pretty sure that ring on your finger suggests *I* asked *you*."

A small smile tipped up my lips. "Okay, so we asked each other. The point is, it's time we took the next step."

His gaze brightened. "Then what's the problem?"

"Me," I answered honestly.

He rubbed his thumbs over the backs of my hands. "You're not a problem, Sunny. A stubborn mule, sometimes, but never a problem. You're a gift, and I treasure you."

"I know, and that's what makes this so hard."

His hands stilled. "You're scaring me, Tink."

"You're not alone," my voice wobbled, "but first, we need to discuss us."

"I thought that was what we were doing?"

"We are, but I mean who we are as individuals, not as a couple. That's why I brought you into my space."

He stared at my charts. "Ahhh," was all he said, but his hesitation and wariness slid back into place.

"Don't worry. I'll be gentle." I patted his hands and then went back to studying my charts.

He just grunted.

"I know you're not a true believer, but please keep an open mind."

"I always do."

"Astrology can tell us a lot about a person, based on the position the planets were in on the day a person was born. There are twelve Zodiac signs, each with its own strengths and weaknesses. When reading someone's horoscope, we can begin to understand who they are as a person, right down to their strengths, weaknesses, likes, dislikes, and more. We can even compare two different signs to see how compatible they truly are."

"Sunny, I don't think—"

I held up my hand. "Open mind, remember? Just hear me out, please."

"Okay."

"Each horoscope sign falls under one of the four Zodiac elements of water, fire, earth and air. You with me?"

"I'm with you."

"Good. I want to make sure you understand the basics before I get into who we are, and more importantly, what our personalities are like."

"No worries. I've got your number." He winked.

"Yes, you do, but that's a whole other topic." I winked back.

"I've got all day." He wagged his eyebrows.

"Focus," I ordered with mock sternness. "Anyway, about the *signs*. People whose signs fall under water elements are overly emotional and sensitive. They are highly intuitive and very mysterious. They usually have a great memory, and love deep conversations and intimacy. They often criticize themselves, and they always support the people they love."

"You are definitely a water sign." He grunted.

I laughed. "Yes, I am. Just as you are a fire sign."

He grinned. "I like the sound of that."

"It's not all glamorous, there, Detective Grumpy Pants. Yes, fire signs are passionate and dynamic, but they are also temperamental. They tend to get mad quickly, but they also forgive easily. Admittedly they are strong and full of energy, leaving others often feeling inspired by their adventurous ways. Always ready for action, they are intelligent, self-aware, creative, and idealistic."

"I can live with that."

"So can I." I gave him a tender smile.

"And fire definitely needs water to keep it from raging out of control, right?" he asked, with hope blossoming in his dark eyes.

"Exactly."

"Then that means we're good together, right?" He beamed.

"Not exactly," I hedged and his face fell. "Many signs fall under the elements, but not all signs are compatible."

He looked alarmed. "Don't tell me you think we shouldn't be together?"

"Actually, every sign *can* be compatible," I quickly amended, "it's just some signs are more compatible than others."

He relaxed a little.

"Now onto the important part. You and me. My sign is Pisces. I am artistic, musical, intuitive, and wise, but I am also compassionate and gentle. Yet I can be overly trusting, a victim or even a martyr, which leads to sadness and being fearful and wanting to escape reality sometimes. We both know I like sleeping and am not a morning person. I like spiritual themes, I don't mind being alone, I love the water, am very visual, and most of all a hopeless romantic. I really don't like people who act like they know everything, I hate being criticized, mistakes I made in the past coming back to haunt me, but most of all cruelty of any kind."

"Yup, that pretty much sums up my girl." He nodded and then his features tightened. "I'm almost afraid to hear about myself."

"Don't worry. I've got your number, too. Less compatible signs can still work, they just require more patience, which is something I have enough of for the both of us."

"Good, because I have plenty of tolerance and acceptance for your little quirks. I'd say we're a match made in heaven."

"Something like that." I smirked and let the word *quirks* slide. "Your sign is Aries. You are determined, courageous, and confident, yet enthusiastic, optimistic, honest, and passionate, which are some of the things I love most about you. Some things not so endearing are your short-tempered, impatient, moody ways. You can be impulsive and aggressive, but only when called for. You tend to like comfortable clothes, but then again, I love seeing you in your NYPD sweats. I love that you take on leadership roles and physical challenges, and your love for sports is so cute. Being delayed annoys you, as well as people who are inactive, or work that doesn't use someone's talent."

"Well, that's not horrible. I mean who wouldn't be annoyed by those things?"

"That's the point. We both have strengths and flaws, but loving someone means loving all of them."

"So, what are you trying to say? Are we or aren't we compatible?"

"Yes, we are, but we have to have the same goals for

our future to be truly happy." I swallowed hard as my gaze met his. "I'm not sure we're on the same page."

"Of course we are! I want to get married and love you for the rest of my life." He narrowed his eyes. "Why, what do you want?"

"A baby."

3

The next morning, I jumped at the chance to run an errand for my mother at Gary's Hardware Store. I needed to keep busy, since Mitch was avoiding *me* now. Ever since I'd told him I wanted a baby, he had been steering clear of me like the plague. At least I didn't have to worry about him pressuring me to pick a wedding date anymore. Work was suddenly super important to him again, and I slid way down his list of priorities.

I knew he was freaking out over the idea of becoming a father. I couldn't blame him, since the thought of being a mother still freaked me out as well, but Jo was right. We'd needed to have this talk before moving forward. I seriously didn't know if this was something he could live with, just as much as I was beginning to suspect it was something I couldn't live without.

I stepped inside of the independent hardware store with its small-town charm, quickly shutting the door behind me. Winter had stormed into Divinity with no warning. A foot of snow had fallen this morning. I brushed off my puffy coat and stomped my boots.

"It's a doozy out there, Gary," I said with a smile.

Gary was a tall, thin man, around forty, who had tight, curly brown hair and a mustache. A good man, he was always helping the locals, and walked with a permanent limp after falling off a ladder while fixing the church gutters. He wore a smile as usual, but it didn't quite reach his eyes today.

"Gonna be a long winter, I'm afraid." He cleared his throat. "Is there something I can help you with?" His gaze kept wandering to the back.

I followed his glance but didn't see anything unusual, so I shrugged. "Yes, actually. My mother wants me to pick up the paint she ordered from you. She says you called and told her it was in."

He checked on his computer and nodded. "She's right, though she might want to wait until the temps get a bit warmer and she can open the windows to air the rooms out."

"I agree, but I'm sure you're getting to know my mother. The word 'wait' is *not* in her vocabulary." I shook my head.

"Right," he responded, half listening to me and still glancing toward the back door.

Something was definitely up. I could have sworn I heard voices back there.

"Is everything okay?"

Just then Cole West came barging in from the back with a puffy, red eye that would be black before long, and knuckles that were scratched and red as well. "It's all taken care of, Gary." He stomped the snow off his work boots and unzipped his Carhartt jacket.

"Oh my gosh, Cole. What happened? Jo is going to flip." I rushed to his side and inspected his eye.

He grabbed my hand gently with his huge palm and lowered it. "I'm fine, Sunny. I was doing some work in the back alley for Gary and tussled with some boxes. That's all." His gaze couldn't seem to quite meet mine.

"Since when did boxes talk?" I moved my face until he had to look at me. "I heard voices, Cole. Who was back there?"

He rubbed his temple. "A blast from my past, trying to catch up with me. I took care of it. That's all you or my wife need to know." He leveled me with a serious expression that would intimidate most, but I knew he was just a big teddy bear beneath all his tattoos and muscles. "She needs to focus on having my babies and nothing else."

I studied him with a hard look of my own. "You don't scare me, Sasquatch." I poked him in his massive chest, and he just grunted. "But for Jo's sake, I agree. She doesn't need any more stress in her life right now, and you don't need any trouble. I thought you were all done with that?" I knew he'd had a shady past, but I'd never really heard the details.

"I am, I promise." He held up his hands. "Trying to be a good citizen, is all, and helping to keep the home of my future children safe." He nodded at me, waved to Gary, and then left the shop with a purposeful stride, not once looking back.

"Alright, Gary, what was that all about?" I crossed my arms and stared him down. Gary opened his mouth, but I held up a hand. "Don't even try to deny something fishy is going on, or I'll never give you another reading again." Gary lived his life according to his horoscope, and visited me weekly. I knew he wouldn't risk it.

His shoulders drooped. "Cole's a great guy."

"I know that, Gary." I put my hands on my hips. "That's why I want to know what he's gotten himself into, so I can help him before he does something stupid."

"He's not going to do something stupid. He really is only trying to keep his town safe. I promise."

"That's what Detective Stone and the Divinity Police Department are for. The last thing we need is some vigilante hero. This isn't a comic strip. It's real life."

"I know, but some enemies require a little something more to keep them in line." Gary actually trembled.

I pursed my lips before finally asking, "What kind of enemy are we talking about?" I had to admit I was more than a little curious. Divinity had been quiet for three whole months. I wasn't sure I could take much more, and admittedly; I was avoiding my own drama.

"The kind Cole used to run around with," Gary responded.

My jaw fell open. "Wait, what? I knew he wasn't exactly an angel in his youth, but I never pictured him as one of the bad guys."

"Cole wasn't always the reliable, steady, gentle giant of a carpenter we all know now. He used to be a prison guard years ago and got messed up with a bad biker gang, doing his fair share of things that he isn't proud of on the wrong side of the law."

"Does he have a record?"

Gary nodded. "But once he met Faith Winslow, he changed his ways. Quit the gang, kept his nose out of trouble, moved to Divinity after the wedding, and changed his profession to the town handyman. He was happy, and he loved her something fierce. After she died, he took it real hard and went a little crazy."

"How crazy?" I asked, wondering if Jo knew any of this. "What did he do?"

"Left town and went back to his old stomping ground. Gunther Corp is the leader of his old gang. He tried to reel Cole back in. I heard it almost worked, too, but Cole came to his senses at the last minute. Some say it was his angel Faith, keeping him on the right track. He nearly killed Gunther. After that, he came back to Divinity but never was the same. Kept to himself and avoided the locals."

"Until Jo set him straight," I said.

"That's right. Jo had been friends with him and Faith both, but Cole shut her out like he did everyone else until you came to town, and well, you know the rest. First comes love, then comes marriage, then comes babies in a baby carriage, and all that." Gary chuckled. "All I can say is I haven't seen Cole this happy in a very long time." Gary's smile faded. "When Gunther showed up in town this morning, I saw the look in Cole's eyes. Fierce and protective and a little crazy."

"He's not going to do anything stupid to jeopardize his new family," I said in Cole's defense. I might not know him as well as Gary, but Jo did. She wouldn't be with anyone who didn't have a good character.

"I hope you're right." Gary sounded grave. "But he's not going to let Gunther stake a claim on Divinity, either. Where Gunther and his gang go, no good follows."

"I'm glad you told me, Gary. I'll be sure to let Mitch know to keep an eye out."

"You do that." Gary nodded, setting ten cans of paint on the counter. "Anything else I can get for you?" he asked, and just like that the conversation was over.

"No, thank you. That will be all." A nagging feeling warned me that *nothing* was over. I had a suspicious feeling I hadn't heard the last of Gunther Corp, and Cole's troubles had only just begun.

———————

THAT AFTERNOON I WAS HEADED INTO NIKKO'S restaurant for a late lunch with Jo and Zoe. The streets were filled with a bunch of people headed to the annual Motorcycle Expo being held at the community center. I bumped into a couple of men in jeans and leather jackets who were standing by the front window. One was only about five-nine, but he was built like a Mack truck, while the other was tall but lean, with scars from a burn on the side of his face.

"Easy there," the tall guy said, as he caught me before I could fall on the icy sidewalk. His hand looked scraped, which made me study him closer and notice the fat lip. "Gotta watch these streets. I already fell once earlier." He smiled as if to put me at ease.

"Streets can be dangerous this time of year," the other guy added with a husky voice. "You take care now."

He tipped his head in my direction, and then started walking down the street away from the restaurant with the other man following closely by his side, their heads tilted as if in conversation. Maybe they were looking for the expo.

"Thank you," I called after them. "I'll have my fiancé, Detective Stone, get the town's road crew to salt the sidewalks. And if you're looking for the expo, keep going another block and turn left at the corner. You can't miss it."

"Thanks," they said with a distracted wave and picked up their pace with purposeful strides, trying to catch up to a third man headed to the expo. The mys-

tery man was too far away for me to see what he
looked like, but when he glanced over his shoulder at
the men in leather, he quickened his steps.

Shrugging, I headed into the restaurant.

Nikko's was an Italian restaurant with an ancient
Italy theme. It competed with our local Greek restaurant called Papa's, but they both did a fabulous business. Divinity loved its history, so most of the
businesses in town had a historical theme. Papa's was
Athens and Nikko's was Tuscany. I couldn't make up
my mind which one I liked better, so I tended to alternate frequenting both. Not to mention, I couldn't cook
to save my life. And since Granny Gert had moved out,
I'd increased their business tenfold. As much as I admired the décor, I knew we weren't here for the
ambiance.

I stepped inside and found Jo at a table right by
the front window. Zoe arrived right after I did and
joined us.

"Okay, what's up?" Zoe asked just as soon as we
had ordered and the waiter had stepped away. "Is it
something with the babies?"

"No, the babies are fine," Jo said evenly. "Their
daddy, not so much." She set her jaw, and I could tell
she was trying to control her anger. "We had a fight,
and he stormed off to the bike expo."

"Oh," I said gravely while nodding. "I mean, oh?" I
blinked innocently after catching their curious stares.

"You know something!" Jo sputtered. "I *knew* it."
She slapped her palm down on the table, rattling our
glasses of ice water.

"Well, you're wrong, because I know nothing." I
shrugged, playing with my napkin and not quite
making eye contact with either of them.

"Yeah, I'm not buying that either." Zoe's tone

sounded so much like Jo's. "We can't take any more drama in this family."

"That's the point," I said helplessly, ready to wring Cole's neck for putting me in this situation.

"If you know something about the black eye my husband came home sporting, please enlighten me," Jo said. "Not to mention his knuckles are swollen something fierce. Not smart when he makes a living by using his hands."

Our waiter came and brought our salads and bread, giving me a moment's reprieve, but it was short-lived. As soon as he left, they stared at me expectantly.

"I ran into him in the hardware store this morning. He tussled with some boxes in the alley. That's all." I quickly repeated what Cole had told me, but I knew they didn't believe that story any more than I had.

"'Tussled,' my big ole' pregnant behind." Jo glared at me. "Sunshine Meadows, I am a strong woman. You of all people know that. I don't need to be protected. I want to know the truth, and I want to know it now."

I groaned then gave up the losing battle. "Someone named Gunther Corp showed up at Gary's Hardware this morning. Cole had words with him in the alley and then told Gary he took care of it, what-ever that means. Gary said Gunther is bad news, and that Cole was just trying to protect you and the town he loves for the sake of all of us and his future children. That really is all there was to it."

Jo's shoulders wilted and her face paled. "That's plenty."

"Who is Gunther Corp?" Zoe asked.

"The leader of Cole's old biker gang," Jo explained. "I've known Cole for a long time. Years ago, we met at the gun range. He has his concealed-carry license for a handgun, while I have my pistol permit. We used to shoot together, and I was friends with his first wife, Faith. She told me she met him when he was a prison guard a couple of towns over and involved with the Rebel Riders."

"Rebel Riders?" Zoe asked.

"They are a biker gang known for their shady dealings and strong-arm tactics with local businesses," Jo said gravely. "With Faith's encouragement, Cole got out, moved here, and became a carpenter. Then she died while riding on the back of his motorcycle. After that, he went dark, taking the blame and looking for ways to punish himself."

"What did he do?" I asked, not sure I wanted to know.

"He doesn't talk about that time in his life except to me. I'm only telling you two because I'm worried about him. He returned to his old gang, but when Gunther was pressuring a liquor store owner to give him a cut of his profits or else, the store owner refused. Gunther planned to burn the place down. That's when Cole knew he needed to walk away, but first he tried to stop Gunther. The fire started anyway while they were fighting. Cole had knocked Gunther out and for a moment, he almost left him there to die. Thankfully he came to his senses and went back for him, but not before Gunther got burned."

My stomach knotted. "Burned?"

Jo nodded. "It was pretty bad. Gunther vowed to seek revenge someday."

I swallowed hard. "Where exactly did Gunther get burned?"

Jo eyed me curiously. "On the side of his face and down his neck and chest, why?"

"I don't think Gunther left town after all."

"What makes you say that?" Zoe asked.

"Because I'm pretty sure I talked to him earlier."

"Where?" Jo asked, looking alarmed.

"Right outside Nikko's front window." I met her gaze and hesitated a moment before adding, "Staring in at your table."

Jo gasped.

"Wow, that's scary. Do you think Gunther will hurt Cole?" Zoe asked.

"Cole is a big man and pretty hard to hurt." Jo squeezed her eyes closed. "I'm more worried Gunther will come after me and the babies, to hurt him where it really counts." Her shoulders trembled in her effort not to cry. "That's why Cole didn't tell me. He knew I would be terrified, but not for myself. I can hold my own, too. I just can't even think about Cole having to go through any more heartache. Gunther won't stop until he gets his revenge."

"That's not going to happen, Jo. You'll see." I patted her hand. "Even Gary said Cole would never let anything happen to his family."

"At what cost?" Jo asked, her eyes filling with tears.

Another disturbing thought came to me. "You said Cole went to the bike expo, right?"

"Yeah. He loves motorcycles."

"He's not the only one," I said, and bit my lip.

"What do you mean?"

"I'm pretty sure that was where Gunther and his sidekick and some mysterious guy they were trying to catch up to were headed over an hour ago." Our lunch had taken longer than normal due to a left-over mess from a large crowd of bikers. My phone buzzed. I checked the caller ID. My stomach pitched. It was Mitch. Knowing I couldn't avoid him forever, I said, "I have to take this. I'll be right back."

I stepped away from our table. "Hi, Mitch. How've you been?"

"We live together, Tink. You see me every day."

"I see you, but I don't really *see* you. Not since I brought up the whole baby thing."

He hesitated, then finally said, "I've been busy with work."

"Yeah, me too." I felt guilty over feeling relieved. Almost just as quickly, I knew we couldn't avoid the topic forever. Taking the plunge, I asked, "Have you given the idea of being a father more thought?" I held my breath.

"I'm working on it, I promise," he said uncomfortably, then cleared his throat. "That's not why I called."

I frowned. "It's not?"

A heavy silence filled the air before Mitch said, "Is Cole with you ladies at lunch?"

"No, why?"

"There's been a murder."

My mouth went dry as a sinking feeling hit me. "Who is it?"

"A man named Gunther Corp."

I let out a noise that didn't even sound human. "How? Where?"

"He was found shot to death in the parking lot of the community center a half an hour ago. No one saw the shooter."

"At the motorcycle expo," I said in barely more than a whisper.

"That's right." Mitch sounded surprised I knew that. "Ballistics isn't back yet, but it appears the murder weapon was a 9-millimeter handgun."

"The same kind of gun Cole owns," I added, feeling numb.

"He was spotted there earlier in a heated argument

with Gunther, but he was gone after the murder happened. I checked his house, but he wasn't there or at Smokey Jo's or at the construction yard."

I explained what happened at the hardware store earlier.

"Any idea where Cole is now?"

"No clue," I mumbled. "Jo is with me. The last place he told her he was going was the expo. He didn't call to say he was going anywhere else. Does this mean what I think it does?" This was going to kill Jo if my hunch was right.

"Unfortunately, yes. At this time Cole West is the number one suspect in the murder of Gunther Corp."

4

M itch, Jo, and I all sat on her living room couch an hour later, trying to figure out what to do. Suddenly the front door opened, and in walked Cole. Biff, his massive Great Dane puppy, charged forward with an awkward gait to greet him.

"Hey, Buddy." Cole caught Biff's front paws as he stood on his hind legs to lick his Daddy's face, no questions asked, just happy to see him.

"Where the hell have you been?" Jo lumbered to her feet just as awkwardly, but she wasn't about to shower him with kisses. She had plenty of questions she wanted answers to like yesterday.

Cole blinked at us in surprise, then focused on his wife with a guilty apologetic expression. "I take it you're still mad at me?"

"Yes, no, I don't know!" She burst into tears.

Cole let go of Biff and rushed to Jo's side. "Awww, baby, don't cry. I'm sorry. It will all be okay, you'll see."

"Maybe not," I muttered.

"What did you do, Cole?" Jo stepped back. "What did you do?"

"I went to the expo just like I said I would, and

then I went for a drive." He looked at her helplessly and a little confused.

"Is that all?" Mitch asked, with a pained but serious expression as he pulled out his notebook.

Cole narrowed his eyes. "Okay, so I ran into a man from my past in the parking lot and we argued."

"And?" Mitch studied him closely.

A muscle in Cole's jaw bulged, and he took a moment as if mentally counting to ten. "And I wanted to hurt him in a bad way. Is that what you want to hear?"

Mitch glanced at me with a worried expression.

"Seriously, guys? I didn't actually hurt him," Cole continued, his gaze shooting between Mitch and myself in disbelief. "I walked away because I knew that is what Jo would want me to do. Then I went for a drive to clear my head. I didn't want to come home and upset Jo more than I already had, so I waited until I cooled off."

"Did anyone see you?" Mitch asked in his most serious detective tone.

"No, no one saw me. I drove through the country." Cole scratched his head, then dropped his hands to his hips, studying us.

"So no one can vouch for your whereabouts?" Mitch carefully asked.

"I don't scare easily, but I gotta admit you're freaking me out, Mitch." Cole's gaze darted around the room. "What the hell's going on?"

Mitch rubbed his jaw and waited a beat before saying, "Gunther Corp is dead."

"What? That can't be right. I just saw him." Cole focused on our expressions as reality sank in. He stumbled back a step, his mouth falling open and eyes wide with shock. "And you think I had something to do with it?"

"I'm just doing my job, Cole," Mitch said carefully. "You were the last person to talk to Gunther before he died, and several witnesses saw you two argue. He was shot point blank with a 9-millimeter handgun."

"I haven't taken my gun out in months." Cole's tone was incredulous.

Mitch made a few more notes. "Where is it now?"

Cole answered in frustration, "In my gun safe."

Mitch's gaze met his with sympathy, but that didn't stop him from doing his job. "Can you show me?"

"Follow me. I've got nothing to hide." Cole led the way to the master bedroom with long purposeful strides and his head held high.

Mitch followed close behind him.

"Are you okay?" I asked Jo after they were out of earshot.

She shook her head. "I don't think so. This is crazy. I know my husband did some questionable things in his past, but he wouldn't hurt anyone." She looked me in the eye with fear and anger and desperation. "And he certainly wouldn't commit murder. You have to believe that, Sunny, you just have to."

"I want to, but I've seen how protective Cole is of you. Are you sure he wouldn't go that far if it came down to protecting you and his babies?"

"Not a chance." Jo's response was immediate. "There was a time Cole did things he wasn't proud of, and I know he can be loud and scary and he hates Gunther, but I'm telling you he's a changed man. He would never risk not being there for his babies. He knows first-hand how it feels to lose a parent. He wouldn't put his children or me through that. You have to help him." She started getting worked up and rubbed her stomach on a wince.

"Shhh, okay, okay." I hugged her. "I promise, Jo. We

will figure this out, but you have to take care of yourself while we do. Your babies need you, too."

"You're right." She took several deep calming breaths while we waited.

Moments later Mitch came back into the living room, wearing a grim expression. Cole followed him with a face that had drained of color. They both stopped and stared at us as if they didn't know what to say.

"It's gone, isn't it?" Jo asked with a hitch in her voice.

Mitch nodded once.

Cole kept shaking his head, looking baffled and confused. "I have no idea where the gun is, and no one knows the combination except for Jo and myself. How could it just disappear? This doesn't make any sense."

"Unless someone's trying to frame you." Mitch nodded, staring off in concentration as though putting the pieces of the puzzle together in his head. "I have to take you in and go by the book, but we're going to figure this out, Cole, you can count on that."

Cole's shoulders wilted and a huge sigh of relief escaped his lips. "Do whatever you have to. I can handle anything as long as I know you believe me."

"Of course, I do," Mitch replied with conviction. "We all do." He squeezed Cole's shoulder, and I held Jo's hand. "But you have to know that doesn't mean the road to proving your innocence is going to be easy."

"That's okay," Cole said, repeating, "I'm okay. It's going to be okay. As long as I know I have you all in my corner, which is something I haven't had much of in my life, then I know I can get through anything."

"So, what do we do now?" Jo asked.

"We get to work," Mitch said, in full detective mode.

Suddenly the mood in the room lightened a little with hope. Maybe everything really would be okay, I thought. But then another scary thought hit me. Maybe it wouldn't...

The real killer was still on the loose.

"Jo sent me with lunch." I walked through the door of West Construction a few days later, carrying a bag with a couple burgers, some French fries, a tub of macaroni and cheese, and a big slice of carrot cake—Cole's favorite.

Cathy, Cole's secretary, was on the phone. She waved me through, indicating Cole was in his office. I waved back at her and made my way inside.

Cole sat behind his desk with a contract spread out before him. It was winter, so business was pretty slow for him, but he needed to keep busy according to Jo. He said he was mulling over some projects for the spring, but she was worried about him. He'd spent every day and evening at the construction yard this week, barely showing his face around town or coming home. She knew it was because he felt ashamed of the man he used to be, and frustrated over the stupid mistakes he'd made recently that had put his family in danger. He was worried what would happen to them if he went to prison. That thought kept him awake at night.

He looked up and smiled at the goodies I brought, but I could see the worry he was trying so hard to hide. He looked tired and a bit thinner upon closer inspection. "You can set it on the desk, Sunny, and tell my wife thanks, would you?"

"Why don't you go home for once and tell her

yourself. Maybe over a nice dinner?" I set the bag on his desk as requested, and then sat down across from him, making it clear I didn't intend to leave until I'd said my piece.

He rubbed a large hand over his buzzed head, drawing his hard eyes together, his lips turning down at the edges. He was so big and strong and tough with his tattoos, chains, and leather. Most people would be intimidated just by looking at him, but Sasquatch had turned into a massive teddy bear. He'd melted like butter in Jo's hands and would do anything for his friends, but anyone who knew him well, knew that he was loyal and fiercely protective to a fault. You didn't mess with him or those he cared about, end of story.

"I've been busy, that's all." He gestured to the papers on his desk then tossed down his pen and sat back.

"I can see that," I said knowingly as I waited patiently.

We both knew there wasn't a thing on his desk so important that required his working overtime. He had a great assistant he trusted enough to hold down the fort after the twins were born, so why not give her more duties now? His family needed him, and he needed them. Besides if he didn't have a clear head, then what good was he to his company?

He held my gaze for a moment longer, but I won. Giving up, he took a deep breath. "What can I say, I just want to keep Jo and our babies safe. She doesn't need the stress that seeing me causes her."

"Are you kidding?" I sputtered. "She's more stressed out over worrying about you because you're shutting her out in trying to protect her. That's not helping either of you, Cole." I reached out and squeezed his hand. "Go home."

He sat in silence for a long minute, then nodded once. "You're right, and I will. I promise. I just want to finish up a few things, then I will be home in time for dinner." He held up his hand. "Don't worry. I'll call her and tell her myself." His lips tipped up into a lopsided smile. "You're good for her, you know. For both of us."

I blinked back tears, feeling so emotional these days. With everything going on, I was pretty much a mess.

"Ditto, Sasquatch," I finally managed to get out, and Cole winked, knowing me almost as well as Mitch did.

Before I embarrassed myself further by becoming a blubbering fool, I thought it best to get while the getting was good and work on my own relationship. I stood up when the door to Cole's office opened. Two men came in, whom I had never seen before, which was a little surprising. Summertime in Divinity was always full of tourists, but this was the middle of winter. The only touristy thing to do in Divinity had been last weekend at the bike expo, but that had ended badly. And after the recent murder in the news, not too many people wanted to come to town right now.

Recognition dawned on Cole's face mixed with surprise, which was quickly replaced with a genuine smile. "I don't believe it. How the hell are you guys?" He stood and shook each of their hands.

I cleared my throat, feeling awkward.

Cole shot me a startled glance as though only now remembering I was still there. "Sorry, Sunny."

He turned to a man who looked to be about his age and almost six feet, with brown curly hair, cut military style short, and a body that had seen better days. It was hard to tell but I was pretty sure he had a prosthetic leg, and one arm was amputated at the elbow.

"This here's Zack Kruger."

"Ma'am." Zack tipped his head in salute.

"Please call me Sunny." I smiled warmly.

"And this guy is my brother-in-law, Miles Winslow," Cole said, his throat sounding clogged.

"*Ex*-brother-in-law actually," the shorter man with blond hair and a slight build replied solemnly, with a nod in my direction.

I acknowledged him with a smile and nod of my own as I stared in wonder over how much he looked like his sister, Faith, from the pictures Jo had shown me of Cole's widow. Jo had said Miles and Faith didn't just look alike. They had been inseparable. Their parents had died when they were young, so they'd only had each other. He'd taken her death especially hard. He'd gone away somewhere no one knew, preferring to heal on his own, and Cole hadn't seen or heard from him since.

I recognized the name Zack Kruger as well. Jo had said the men had been the Three Musketeers from the moment they met. After Cole married Faith and moved to Divinity, Miles had followed them, working for Cole while Zack went into the army. Zack hadn't been able to come home for the funeral, as he was deployed in Afghanistan, and Miles had ventured off on his own soon after the burial.

"You'll always be my brother." Cole clapped Miles on the shoulder.

Miles nodded, his face flushing with emotion as his Adam's apple bobbed. "That's why we're here, man. We heard about what happened."

Zack nodded gravely, looking concerned. "You okay?"

"I've been better." Cole's face strained as he looked Zack over. "I take it you got out early with honorable discharge. What the hell happened, man?"

Zack shoved his good hand in his jean's pocket. "War."

"I'm sorry."

"Me too, but I'll live."

Miles looked at Zack and then at Cole with promise and conviction in his eyes. "What can we do to make sure *you* have a life."

"You're already doing it," I interrupted, hoping to dissuade any of them from taking matters into their own hands. That was the last thing Mitch or Cole needed. "My fiancé, Detective Stone, is working on clearing Cole's name."

"Wait a minute. Isn't that the detective who arrested him?" Zack eyed me suspiciously with a hard gaze.

"Protocol," I quickly tried to reassure him. "He was just doing his job and going by the book, but that doesn't mean he won't do everything possible to make sure Cole stays a free man."

"It's okay, guys. Mitch is a friend," Cole said with confidence.

"Sounds it," Miles added, heavy skepticism lacing his voice.

"I know you're just trying to protect Cole, but you're not the only one who has his best interest in mind. His pregnant wife is also *my* best friend. You can rest assured that none of us want to see her raise her babies alone."

"I heard you were going to be a father." Miles smiled at Cole, but I could tell it pained him to do so. It didn't take being psychic to know he was hurting. If his sister was all he had, then he would never have a niece or a nephew to spoil and love and help raise. He shifted and slipped his hands in his coat pockets. "Congratulations. I hope everything works out for you."

"Yeah, congrats, man. You deserve to be happy. You've been through a lot." Zack looked down to the floor as if uncomfortable with emotion. After all he had been through himself, it wasn't surprising.

"We all have." Cole nodded. "Thanks guys. You stopping by means more than you know. Don't take so long next time."

"I agree, it's been too long, and far too much has happened. Life has a way of getting in the way sometimes. You just say the word if you need anything, you hear?" Zack's voice rang with sincerity.

"No worries, brother," Miles added. "We're not going anywhere until this mess is settled and justice is served."

5

"**O**kay, so where are we at?" I asked as I walked into Divinity Police Department later that day.

Mitch's office had stark white walls, a desk, a couple chairs, and blinds on the windows. No personal touches for safety reasons, but things went beyond that with Mitch. He tended to keep the world at bay, not liking to talk about his past. I had broken down many of his walls, but he didn't even let *me* in fully. And that was another thing we needed to work on.

Today was Friday. I'd kept my nose out of the case for longer than I had thought possible, mostly because I had been busy cheering Jo up and talking my mother off the ledge while she was making her inn repairs and dealing with my father's bucket list and Granny Gert being "helpful." Talking to Mitch was the least of all evils right now. Besides, it had been long enough for the police to have figured out which direction they were headed in. And if they hadn't, then they would need my consulting services.

I wanted to help even if it meant working side-by-side with Mitch. Funny how you could live with someone yet manage to hardly see them, but working a case together meant no escape from each other's company. *No escape* was something we both needed in order to deal with the elephant in the room that was threatening our future.

Mitch sat in the chair behind his desk with all sorts of notes and pictures spread out before him. He didn't look any better than Cole, with his hair all messy, his clothes wrinkled, and the crow's feet at the corners of his eyes deep with fatigue. He raised his head and stared at me with stormy gray eyes full of too many emotions for him to hide. His wide, full lips remained unsmiling, and a muscle in his whiskered jaw pulsed once beneath the long, jagged scar. He didn't say a word, but he didn't have to.

The look in his eyes said it all.

In some cases, I had been too close to be of any help. In others, he had. This time it didn't have anything to do with that. We were both equally close to Jo and Cole. No, this time it was personal. He didn't want me working with him because work was his way of avoiding talking to me, same as Cole had done with Jo.

Admittedly, I had allowed Mitch to get away with it because it was easier to go on as if nothing was different between us, and avoid the conversation altogether, but that would never do. We couldn't get married if we weren't on the same page, and neither one of us wanted to risk ending what we had built. What we had come to cherish. What we'd fought so hard to hang on to. The problem was we couldn't stay engaged forever. At some point we had to either move forward or end things.

But that day would not be today.

I missed my best friend. Smiling tenderly, I walked

over and took his face in my hands, then leaned down and kissed him full on the lips. "Hi, Mitch."

He smiled back tentatively, looking more relieved than he'd probably intended, but that was okay. We both needed this. "Hi, Sunny." He pulled me down on his lap and wrapped his arms around me, resting his head on mine. "I've missed you," he whispered.

"We still have to talk."

"I know. Can we focus on clearing Cole's name first?"

"Okay."

"Yeah?" He sounded so surprised and filled with hope, as if a huge weight had been lifted from his shoulders.

My heart melted. "Yeah," I replied, turning my head and kissing him deeper this time, with everything I felt but couldn't seem to say.

Mayor Cromwell, Chief Spencer, and Captain Walker came into the room and caught us embracing. My eyes widened as I broke off the kiss, and I felt my cheeks flush crimson. I quickly stood up. Mitch shot me a conspiratorial wink, and then focused on the men, transforming into Detective Stone, aka all business.

"Are you alright, Miss Meadows?" Mayor Cromwell shot Mitch an evil glare. The short, stocky man who looked like a wild, red-headed troll had never liked the detective, but he adored me. A true believer, he came to my office regularly for a reading.

"I'm fine." I smiled wide, smoothing a hand down the front of my sweater and peasant skirt. "You all just startled me."

"I can see that." Chief Spencer, who was an older version of Mitch, looked me over with disdain. He, on the other hand, was *not* a fan of me.

"Well, now that we're all recovered, let's try to figure out what we're doing here, shall we?" Captain Walker, who liked *both* of us, came to the rescue, thank goodness. He was tall and lean, with a bald head, a gray goatee, and about as fine a cop as there was. His only downfall was that he had a huge sweet tooth. He polished off the last of Granny Gert's cookies with a satisfied grin as he closed the door behind him.

Granny Gert was *his* number one fan.

"The last thing we need is for the Rebel Riders to pick up where their leader Gunther Corp left off and start leaning on our local business owners." Mayor Cromwell heaved his stocky frame into a chair and shook his head. "Divinity can't take any more bad publicity."

"I'm more concerned about my kids being safe." Chief Spencer crossed his arms and leaned against the wall. "I'm all for standing by our own, but what do we really know about Cole West, other than he does fine work?"

"I can vouch for Cole, Chief," Mitch said.

"I hate to say this, but can you really, Mitch?" Captain Walker interjected.

"If he can't, I can," I piped in. "I know Cole doesn't have an alibi, and he certainly has motive, and his gun is missing. But we don't know for sure that his gun is the gun that killed Gunther. What we do know is that Cole is the husband of Joanne Burnham, and we *all* know Jo. She is a great judge of character and would never marry—let alone bear the children of—a man who was capable of murder. I think we need to trust our gut on this one and find the evidence we need to clear his name."

"I think you're right," Captain Walker agreed, and

for the first time since I entered Mitch's office, I breathed a sigh of relief.

"Then where do we start?" Chief Spencer responded.

"Well, I think we start with the deceased. Who did Gunther have as enemies?" Mitch thumbed through his notes. "For instance, who was Ray Simone? We know he was his right-hand man, but what else was he? All I know for sure is he was in town and with Gunther right up until the afternoon he died."

"Then I say we start with him." Chief Spencer looked around the room as if he dared anyone to say otherwise.

I had to bite back a grin. He might not like me, but I loved him for always having my fiancé's back. Mitch could do no wrong in his eyes, and that was fine by me.

"I agree," I chimed in, but only got a narrowed suspicious glance in response.

"Thanks, babe," Mitch said, and I could have kissed him right then and there. He shot me a look full of gratitude and promises to come. "I'm pretty sure Simone has left town, but first thing tomorrow morning, I will talk to him."

"So long as you take Miss Meadows with you," Mayor Cromwell interjected, not one to be left out.

Mitch looked at me with a penetrating gaze as he answered with, "I wouldn't have it any other way."

MITCH AND I PULLED INTO THE PARKING LOT OF THE Divinity Hotel later that day. Since my mother's inn wasn't open for business quite yet, we figured we would start looking for Ray at the only hotel in town.

Divinity was an old-fashioned town with big Victorian homes and businesses that showcased different eras throughout history. There were newer buildings popping up here and there as the town grew and evolved, but the older buildings held tight to history and tradition, resisting change of any kind.

This hotel was one of the oldest businesses—a large brick building a few stories high, with a patio on the rooftop so the tourists could watch the seasonal parades and festivities down below. The hotel itself was small but quaint, decorated in an Art Deco style from the 1930's, which was inspired by the artists of Paris.

We walked through the front door into the streamlined, polished look of the lobby. There were pieces of lacquered wood furniture, combined with brushed steel, and lined with exotic Zebra skin upholstered material scattered about the lobby. Exotic green and orange starburst motifs with small amounts of black and gold arranged in geometric shapes covered the floors and walls.

The fireplace was the focal point of the room. A combination of oak, walnut, and mahogany was used to create the mantel, because these types of wood were easy to carve. The contrasting grains of each wood only added to the design. A beveled mirror was built right into the center of the design, surrounded by hand-painted tiles, while carved beading, flowers, and leaves lined the frieze.

Chuck Webb owned the hotel. He was a stocky man of about fifty, with brown hair cut military-style. He'd had a problem with alcohol, but his wife, the younger Abigail Brook—who used to have a crush on Mitch—had married and reformed the hardened man. She'd blessed him with a baby girl, and the darling child had her daddy wrapped around her sweet little finger. I clung to the fact that if someone like Chuck could come to adore fatherhood, then there was hope for Mitch as well.

Abby and I would never be friends, but we'd been through a lot together and had become amicable acquaintances. I was thrilled for her that she'd finally found her happy ending. I smiled and waved as she stood behind the front desk with the baby in her arms, and a pang of longing hit me unexpectedly. My throat clogged up with emotion, making it hard to swallow, and I actually had to blink back tears.

"You okay?" Mitch asked, as we approached the desk.

I nodded, pointing to my throat. "I swallowed my gum by accident," I managed to get out.

He nodded his understanding, accepting my excuse without hesitation. Either he genuinely believed my explanation or he understood the real reason behind my reaction, by the way I'd been staring at that precious bundle of joy, and this was yet another avoidance tactic. Fine by me. I couldn't handle a conversation of that nature at the moment any more than he could.

"Hi Abby. You look great." I pasted on a pleasant smile. "Motherhood agrees with you. She's getting so big."

Abby beamed, her mousy brown hair and no makeup a thing of the past ever since her cousin had given her a makeover, which had done wonders for her confidence. "Thanks, and I know, right? Don't blink or they're off to college. That's what everyone says. I never believed them, but she's growing so quickly every single day. Time is going by so fast. I'm trying to enjoy every second."

"Congratulations, Mrs. Webb." Mitch eyed the baby with a mixture of wariness and horror, dashing whatever sliver of hope I had felt moments ago. He cleared his throat. "Is your husband around?" He swiftly changed the subject.

"Sure thing, Detective. I'll get him from the back." Abby disappeared inside the office behind the desk.

Shortly after, Chuck walked out, leaving Abby and the baby behind. He had a protective look on his face as he stared suspiciously at Mitch. "Detective Stone, I can't say I'm happy to see you, as seeing you usually involves trouble. I can assure you I'm an honest man now. I have my Abby to thank for that."

"I have no doubt about that, Mr. Webb." Mitch pulled out his notebook. "This visit doesn't concern you personally."

"Congratulations, by the way," I interjected with a sincere smile. Sometimes Mitch didn't have a clue.

Chuck's whole face lit up. "Thank you, Miss Meadows. I'm truly blessed."

"Yes, you are. Why, I was just telling Mitch—"

"That we need to act quickly before this town is turned upside down with locals and outsiders wanting answers," Mitch cut me off, his meaningful stare screaming, *Stay focused and keep this investigation on track, Tink!*

"Ah, I heard about that biker gang leader named Gunther Corp getting shot. Can't say it's a shame. I heard he was demanding money from local businesses in exchange for his protection. Or in other words, in exchange for him not trashing their place."

"He definitely wasn't a stand-up guy, that's for sure, but no one deserves to be murdered. It's my job to find his killer."

"Good luck to you. All I know is, as a local businessman myself, I couldn't have afforded paying him off to make him leave me alone."

"Did he make threats to you?" Mitch asked, with a fair amount of suspicion in his tone as he jotted down a few notes.

"No, thank God, and even if he had, I'm not a killer. And just in case you don't believe me, I have an alibi for that day during the bike expo. I was here the whole time, dealing with a full hotel."

"No one's accusing you of anything," I hastily reassured Chuck, shooting Mitch a glance that said, *You might not like babies, but chill out, Grumpy Pants, or we won't get any information, and then your best friend will be screwed!*

"Good, because the last thing I or my family need to worry about is to go through being a suspect in a murder investigation again. We have our daughter to think about now, and that's all either of us is concerned with." His voice rang with sincerity. "Besides, as far as I know, Gary's Hardware was the only business hit."

My gaze met Mitch's. As much as I liked Gary, desperation could make a man do things he would never normally do. I wasn't letting Cole West take a fall for anyone, no matter how stand-up the guy normally was.

"I'll look into that." Mitch made another note in his book. "In the meantime, what can you tell us about Ray Simone?"

"Well, he stayed here at the hotel. Corp never did. Not sure where he stayed, but Simone seemed more of a solo act. When they were together, they acted like they were a team. Yet after Corp was murdered, Simone didn't seem upset in the least. And he never pressured me for anything. Just before he checked out, I heard him on the phone telling someone to round up the Rebel Riders for a meeting, like he was the new man in charge or something. He said something about there were going to be some changes."

Mitch sent me a look, and I knew we were on the same page. If Ray was the new leader, maybe he had killed Gunther and tried to pin it on Cole to make that happen. That was motive, and he certainly had access. He claims to have gone to the men's room before joining Gunther outside, only to find him dead, but no one could verify that. Ray was the one to call the police, but that didn't mean anything. He never personally pressured any businesses, and kept his distance in where he stayed, almost as if he knew Gunther was going to die and didn't want to be linked to the crime in any way.

"Did he say where he was going when he left?" Mitch asked.

"No, but he left pretty quickly, like he didn't want to risk being brought in for questioning or anything. I'm guessing he probably went back to whatever hellhole he came from to lie low. And to rally his gang."

"Thank you, Mr. Webb." I held out my card, and Mitch raised an inky black eyebrow to which I ignored. "Give me a call if you can think of anything else."

"Will do."

Mitch and I walked outside and stopped on the sidewalk. "Well, what now, Boss?" I smiled up at him, knowing exactly how to play the game.

He stared down at me. "So *now* I'm the one in charge?"

"Of course." I fluttered my lashes innocently.

He just shook his head on a slight grin. "I know a

detective in Stillwater. That's the town the Rebel Riders are based out of. I'll give him a call."

"Why call, it's so impersonal and not nearly as effective."

He narrowed his eyes at me. "As effective as what?"

"Road trip," I hollered, and jumped into the passenger seat of his car.

"That's what I was afraid you were going to say."

6

Saturday morning, we left bright and early for the Stillwater Police Department. Stillwater was another small town, much like Divinity, about an hour away up north. Northern New York wasn't as strictly policed as central New York. The further you got away from the Big Apple, the more remote things became.

Gunther had been an inmate when Cole first met him back in his wild and reckless days. Now that we knew a little more about Gunther, it had only been a matter of time before he caught up with Cole again to seek his revenge.

"Any luck on finding Cole's gun?" I asked from the passenger seat of Mitch's car, holding my hands out in front of the heater to warm them up. Lake-effect snow was falling in big fat flakes the farther north we drove.

"No." Mitch sounded bleak. He ran a hand through his curls, still damp from his morning shower, and sighed. "With no alibi and plenty of motive, the only thing saving him is the missing murder weapon. At this point I almost hope it doesn't turn up. At least until we find some more leads."

"Hey, wait, you just passed the police station!" I

watched the building disappear through his back window.

"We're not going to the station."

"How come?"

"Detective Torres is in the mood for coffee," Mitch's eyes met mine, "and a little privacy."

"Interesting. What do you think it means?"

"That whatever he has to say, he doesn't want his coworkers hearing."

We didn't speak again until we reached our destination on the outskirts of town. Mitch pulled up in front of a small diner and cut the engine. Given that the weather was terrible and this place was off the map, it was pretty much dead. Mitch led the way inside, and I followed. The diner was small but cozy, and the aromas of eggs, bacon, and syrup filled the air. We came to a stop at a corner booth and sat down across from a tough looking man with thick, black, slicked-back hair, and a dark goatee.

"Detective Torres, this is Sunny Meadows, a consultant to the Divinity Police Department."

"Nice to meet you, Ms. Meadows. Please call me Juan." He set down his cup of steaming coffee and held out his hand.

I slid my palm against his and shook while smiling wide, liking him already. "Likewise, Juan, and it's Sunny to you."

The waiter came by and Mitch ordered black coffee and a western omelet with a side of sausage and toast, reminding me Granny Gert no longer lived with us. The poor man was starving unless he ate out. I, on the other hand, was too nervous to eat. I ordered a cup of chamomile tea, wishing it would settle my stomach. All my hopes were riding on this visit, praying for a new lead.

"Juan is undercover in the Gang Investigations Unit here in Stillwater." Mitch took a sip of his coffee. "I went through the academy with Juan in the city. We go way back. Isn't that right, Juan?" Mitch shoveled a forkful of omelet into his mouth and groaned.

"Absolutely." Juan eyed Mitch curiously as he ate like he'd just gotten off a season of Survivor. "We were both a part of the Homicide Unit before my *partner* bailed on me for the small-town life." Juan let a mock scowl transform his face before growing serious. "He's one hell of a cop, but I get why he had to leave." Juan's gaze locked onto Mitch's, and Mitch nodded once with obvious emotion. Juan focused back on me. "I switched to the Gangs Unit, but I never thought I'd end up in this neck of the woods. We've been after the Rebel Riders for a while now. I know all about Gunther Corp and Ray Simone."

"We were hoping you would say that." I pulled out my own notebook and pen, earning an amused smirk from Mitch. "What can you tell us about Ray?"

"Well, he joined the gang a few years back. He has a record, mostly juvie stuff—a few misdemeanors, petty larceny, not really that big of a deal. Gunther was the badass. He'd been in and out of jail on felonies for most of his life, but he knew how to work the system. The gang had been putting a lot of pressure on local businesses, but none of the business owners would press charges. Those who did felt defeated. Nothing ever came of it, so 'why bother' became the common attitude."

"You think he has someone on the inside?" Mitch asked with a frown.

"Internal Affairs has been investigating our office. Officer Adam Burrows works the beat that a lot of the businesses are on. He claims not to know anything, but my guess is he's been turning a blind eye to a lot that's been going down in Stillwater for a cut of the action."

"Really?" I asked. "What are you thinking?"

"Rumor has it the man likes to gamble and he likes women, both of which are expensive hobbies." Juan looked around the restaurant before continuing. "Once IA got involved, things calmed down for a while, then suddenly the Rebel Riders moved on to Divinity. Corp probably got sick of waiting for the green light from Burrows, but Adam wouldn't like missing out on any action if he needed the money. Not to mention Corp could bring Burrows down with him if it came to that. Adam just might have been desperate enough to do something about that."

"Do you think he was in Divinity at the time of the murder?" Mitch asked.

"My guess is yes, since he called in sick the day of the murder. You might want to check into that."

Mitch made a note then met Juan's gaze. "What about Simone? Any news of him? He left Divinity pretty quickly."

"I heard he's back in Stillwater. Doesn't surprise me. It was common knowledge that he wanted to be the leader of the Rebel Riders."

"Did he want it badly enough to kill Gunther to get it?" I chimed in before sipping my tea.

"It's hard to say." Juan took a sip of his coffee. "Gunther treated Ray like he was nothing, even though he was second in command. That has to wear on a man over time. Not to mention Gunther was becoming increasingly unstable. Taking chances. Making mistakes. My sources say a lot of the gang were getting tired of it."

"Know where we can find Burrows or Simone?" Mitch asked.

"Well, the gang's turf is on the east side of town, and where the gang is, Burrows tends to follow. Though I have to say they've all been lying low. Not sure how much more info you'll find. Careful out there, buddy. Weather's nasty, and it's not gonna get any better."

"Thanks, Juan." Mitch drained the last of his coffee, stood, and held out his hand. "I've been through worse."

"Roger that." Juan stood as well, and shook hands. "Anytime, partner. Though it looks like you've got a new partner these days to help you through the storm."

"Sure do, and she's a whole lot better looking than my old one." Mitch winked.

"I can't argue with you there." Juan chuckled and gave me a smile.

I blushed to the roots of my pale blond hair over Mitch's compliment.

"In all honesty, it was a pleasure to meet you, Sunny." Juan bowed gallantly.

"The pleasure's all mine," I replied with sincerity. Anyone who brought out the lighter side of my fiancé was a treat to be around. "Can you let us know if you learn anything new?" I handed him my card.

"Will do." He grinned at Mitch and held my card up as if it were a trophy. "Look who's got her number now."

"And I've got yours." Mitch pointed at him with a mock scowl, slipped his arm around me possessively, and guided me out of the diner, calling over his shoulder. "She's already taken."

Detective Torres laughed behind us every step of the way.

HOURS LATER WE CRUISED AROUND THE EAST SIDE OF Stillwater for the umpteenth time without much luck. Normally I didn't like male bravado and all that, but I had to admit, a warmth had infused my every cell when Mitch had staked his claim on me. No matter how archaic it might be, it had felt fabulous. But that incredible warmth had faded as Juan's prediction came true. The weather didn't get any better, it got worse. The plows weren't able to keep up with the rate the snow was falling, and the roads were a mess.

"This is nuts. I'm cold, I'm tired, and I'm hungry. I don't know how you do this on a daily basis." I pouted in the seat beside Mitch.

"You should have eaten at the diner," Mitch replied, as if talking to a child.

"I wasn't hungry then." I knew my tone was whiny, but I couldn't help it. My name was Sunny for a reason —I was full of sunshine and warmth. I hated the snow and cold.

"And now we're on the case when it's not convenient to stop and eat," my fiancé pointed out, ever the logical being.

"I can't help that," I grumbled, knowing I probably sounded like a child. I was not being a very good partner right about now, but a big part of me knew my whining didn't have anything to do with this case. It had everything to do with our unresolved issues that were really starting to get to me.

"And I can't help that a lead didn't pay off." Mitch

looked at me helplessly. "Welcome to police work, Miss Meadows."

"Funny." I scowled.

"I try." He smirked.

"Any chance you can try harder?" I looked over at him with the utmost sincerity, all traces of kidding aside.

He rubbed the back of his neck, then finally responded, "Alright, let's call it a day and go get some linner."

I wrinkled my nose. "Linner?"

"Well, brunch is breakfast and lunch. We're *way* beyond that, but we're not quite at dinner. I figure linner must be lunch and dinner."

"I take it back. Seriously," I snorted, "you're so not funny."

"I know, but I repeat. At least I try." This time he was the one to sound sincere.

I softened with a tender smile on my face and a heart full of love for this complex man. As much as we kidded around and as many hurdles as we had to overcome, I couldn't imagine my life without him. "And I love you for it." I blew him a kiss.

His gaze locked on mine, but he didn't say the words back. My smile faded as uncertainty set in once more. Would love be enough for us, or would I indeed have to learn to live without the love of my life? Mitch gunned the car to do a U-turn, and it started to slide. I squealed, grabbing onto the bar above my head, and he cursed as he fought to bring her under control to no avail. We spiraled until we slid off the road, coming to a stop in the ditch.

"Oh!" I slapped my hands on the dash. "Oh, my. What now, boss?" I looked around helplessly. What the heck had all that been about?

He clenched his jaw on a wince and smacked the steering wheel once, then responded without giving anything away, "Now we call for help."

Ten minutes of awkward silence later, a tow truck came to help.

A big burly man stepped out of the truck and started walking toward us. If I didn't know he was here to help, I would be terrified. He had a bald head, a big bushy beard remnant of the band ZZ Top, and a big belly, but his massive height made up for it. In fact, I was pretty sure this guy was taller than Sasquatch. I shot a glance in Mitch's direction, looking for reassurance. When his eyes widened and mouth fell open, my stomach dropped.

Mitch cleared his throat and climbed out of the car, while I followed his lead. He held out his hand. "Detective Stone," he said, emphasizing the *detective* part. My fiancé was anything but stupid. The snow fell even harder now, dusting our clothes immediately. I felt like we were in the middle of a snow globe. Normally, I thought those were beautiful... now, not so much.

"Ralph Peters." The man grasped Mitch's hand with his huge paw and shook hard. I had to give Mitch credit. He didn't so much as wince. "It's a doozy out here. Gotta watch these roads this far north, though I have to say, your car's stuck in here good. Looks like you spun her out, almost as if you were avoiding something." He looked around the empty road and scratched his beard.

"Oh, he was avoiding something, all right," I muttered beneath my breath, but Mitch heard, judging by the stiffening of his shoulders.

"My foot slipped, and I hit the gas," Mitch responded, with a tone that brooked no argument.

"You're not from these parts, are you, Detective?" Peters reached under the car and hooked a chain up to it. "I've lived here all my life. I'd know if you were," he added as he stood and eyed Mitch curiously. "What brings you 'round these parts?"

"Official business. Since you obviously know everything that goes on in this town, I'm sure you've heard that Gunther Corp was murdered."

Everything about the monster of a man changed. His curious amicable expression hardened, his muscles stiffened, and his eyes filled with hate. "No offense, but I say good riddance."

"None taken, but why would you say that? Was Mr. Corp not well liked around these parts?"

"He was the leader of the Rebel Riders. He got off on terrorizing pretty much everyone in town."

"Except you."

"Do I look like I scare easily?" The giant's face was hard and unsmiling.

"No, I can't say that you do."

"Corp knew better than to mess with me. Problem was he didn't know enough not to mess with my wife."

Mitch studied the man. "Did he harm her?"

"Not physically, but he preyed on her emotions and seduced her." A muscle in Peter's jaw bulged.

"Last I checked, it takes two to tango." Mitch watched him intently.

"And only one to commit murder," Ralph growled.

"Are you confessing to the crime, Mr. Peters? Maybe you found out they were having an affair and killed him for it."

I sucked in a breath. Was Mitch nuts? He had to know he was playing with fire by baiting the man.

"And maybe this cold has addled your brain, Detective." Ralph clenched and unclenched his fists. "Why would I stay in town if I committed murder?"

Mitch shrugged, donning an innocent expression. "Stranger things have happened."

"I suggest you get someplace warm and thaw out so you can start thinking straight again." Ralph unhooked the chain from Mitch's car. "Will you look at that? The darn thing broke." He threw it in the back of his tow truck before letting us see.

"Wait, where are you going?" I asked, ready to throttle Detective Stone in the name of justice.

"You'll have to call someone else," Peters said over his shoulder, not looking back even once as he revved the engine.

"Why would a tow truck driver not have extra supplies on his truck?" Mitch hollered after him suspiciously.

Ralph turned around long enough to shrug innocently, but there was a definite sparkle in his eye as he replied, "Stranger things have happened, Detective," and then he was gone.

7

"Well, I have to say it's a cold day in hell." Mitch zipped his black leather jacket up all the way as we stood outside the front door of the inn.

I had to agree. It had been freezing the past twenty-four hours, and we'd definitely gone through hell after Peters had left us in the ditch. It had taken forever to get someone else to pull us out, and by then it was too dark and the weather too bad to drive home to Divinity. The only place that had a room in Stillwater was a dive of a motel, but we had made do.

Only to return home this morning to no groceries in the house, a missing Morty, and a heater on the fritz. But who was I kidding? I knew the "cold day in hell" Mitch was referring to was when I suggested we go to the inn and beg for mercy. It might not be open for business while my mother remodeled, but they had plenty of room and people who knew how to cook. Besides, neither one of us could face Jo and Cole, and there was no place else to go. These were desperate times, and I wasn't too proud to admit it.

"Ha ha. I have to say I miss my family. Or at least

Granny, anyway. I *will* learn to cook if life ever calms down, I promise."

"I'm not marrying you for your cooking, Tink." He winked down at me with a soft smile tipping up the corners of his lips.

A little thrill zipped through me over his words, and the look full of promise blazing in his dark eyes. And a small voice whispered he might not be marrying me at all if he didn't want children. I decided to keep our truce and block out the voice for now. We would have to deal with it eventually, but I planned to wait until the whisper became a roar.

"Really, now? I can't imagine what skills I could possibly possess that would be worth marrying me over." I blinked up at him innocently, but I couldn't quite hide the twinkle in my eyes.

"Maybe I'll have to refresh your memory."

"If you're lucky, maybe I'll show you just exactly how talented I am."

My mother chose to open the door right as I was speaking. A perfectly plucked eyebrow crept up into her artfully styled, golden blond hairline. "Talents? And what would those be, darling?"

I tried not to grind my jaw. "Fortune-telling, Mother. I thought maybe I could read yours and see how well this place is going to do for you?"

"Surely you jest!" My mother brushed a hand over her paint-splattered coveralls, managing to make them look like designer wear. "My sweet child, I have exquisite taste. This town is going to adore what I have planned."

"This town isn't New York City, Mom. I just don't want you disappointed if your new business venture doesn't work out exactly as you plan."

"I'm not worried. I have lots of help." She harrumphed. "Not so much from your father and Harry. I fear the grounds will never be the same, but I'll deal with that when spring comes. And Granny and Fiona still haven't quite mastered the art of cohabitating peacefully, but at least they have help now. All I can say is, thank goodness for Sally and Frank. At least I can count on the inn being clean and nothing breaking down."

"As interesting as this conversation is, Mrs. Meadows," Mitch said with a shiver, "would it be too much to ask if we might come in?"

"Of course, you can," my father boomed as he joined my mother in the doorway. "Vivian, where are your manners?"

"They've gone ice fishing with your sanity apparently," she muttered all flustered-like, and for the first time I realized she wasn't as confident as she tried to act.

Dad pushed the door wide open so Mitch and I could walk through with our overnight bag. "Honeymoon over already?" Dad chuckled. "Don't tell me our fine detective here is returning you to your family. All sales are final with this one, as she's about to expire." My father winked at me.

"Cute, Dad, but Vicky is *my* house, remember? I would be the one returning Detective Stone, which I have no intention of doing anytime soon."

"Thanks, I think," Mitch chimed in, and closed the door behind us, adding, "Heater's on the fritz and the fridge is pretty empty. Any chance we can stay here for the night? I have a call in to a friend who agreed to fix it first thing in the morning."

"Of course, you can stay." My mother searched the area. "Might as well have the whole family together. Morty's around here somewhere."

"Morty's here and you're not shrieking in terror?" I stared in shock. *Wow, hell really had frozen over.*

"I'm not saying we're best buddies or anything, but we've formed a sort of truce after he saved my life." She hoisted a thin shoulder, acting like it was no big deal, but I knew better. She'd softened toward him, and he'd accepted her. "Besides, we both know that cat of yours does what he wants to anyway, so why fight it."

"That's true," I responded, and just like that, Morty appeared from out of nowhere, wearing a snowflake bowtie.

Granny Gert must have made him a new one, since I was slacking in that department as well, after promising I would keep him outfitted properly after she left. I couldn't cook, couldn't clean, and couldn't clothe my fur baby. Who was I kidding? I was beginning to doubt what kind of mother I would make. I chewed my bottom lip.

"There you are, you little stinker." I reached down to scratch him behind the ears, and he flinched.

Morty never flinched.

My gaze shot to Mitch's, and he looked just as confused as I was. "Morty skittish. That's a first."

And now I've made my cat jumpy. Morty stared hard at me, then turned up his nose at Mitch as he walked away, though he stumbled and wobbled a bit before disappearing out of the room.

"Skittish and unsteady." I pursed my lips. "What did you do to him, Mother?"

She scoffed. "Absolutely nothing. He hasn't acted like this all morning. Not until you arrived, my dear. If anyone's to blame, it's clearly you."

"Now, now. No one's to blame. He's probably just getting old," my father reasoned.

"Aren't we all," Fiona added, as she came into the living room from the kitchen.

"Speak for yourself," Granny Gert responded, as she sashayed along behind her.

"Boys oh day, I'd say I have you all beat," said a little old pear-shaped woman with tight gray curls. She was hunched over as she bustled about the room in polyester pants and a paisley printed blouse with a brightly colored half-apron tied about her waist.

"This is my granddaughter Sunny, and her beau, Mitchel Stone." Granny Gert pointed to us. "And this here is our new cook, Great-Grandma Tootsie," she said with a flourish, just as proud as punch. "She's ninety-nine years old. Can you believe it? I hired her myself." Granny's snappy brown eyes sparkled with mischief. "Don't let her age fool ya. She's just as spry and sharp of the mind as anyone I know. Why, I wouldn't be surprised if she outlived us all."

"Oh, go on with you now." Great-Grandma Tootsie waved her hand about, but her smile was pure gold and her faded blue eyes filled with pleasure.

"I agree, her cooking's amazing, but don't ask her for the recipe. All you'll get is, 'Oh, I just use a little bit of this and a pinch of that'," Fiona teased, and it was clear the three had already become fast friends. Looked like the Dynamic Duo had become the Tasty Trio of the inn.

"I can't see that well—immaculate degeneration and all—but I don't need to." Great-Grandma Tootsie straightened as much as she could to show her pride. "Why, I've been cooking for so long, I guess I just know what's what."

"I have to say, I was skeptical at first," my mother admitted to the room, "but Toots has definitely proven me wrong. Age has nothing to do with art, and my kitchen needs her."

"You heard the boss, ladies," Great-Grandma Tootsie said to Granny Gert and Fiona. "Let's shake and bake. We've got a lunch to prepare." They hustled out of the room without a single argument, with Toots trailing in their wake, humming big band show tunes every step of the way.

I stared at my mother, my mouth hanging open, having no idea what to say.

"Strange, I know," my mother responded anyway. "But the price is right. She wants to work for free. Says she has plenty of money, and this will keep her young. She's outlived all but one granddaughter, who moved to Florida after turning sixty, and one great-granddaughter, who is forty and single in New York City. They tried to get her to join them, but apparently Toots doesn't like to fly and wants to keep her feet firmly planted where her roots are, in upstate New York. How could I say no? I guess we're her new family now." My mother left to clean up her paint supplies, calling over her shoulder for us to pick any room and make ourselves at home. Everyone else had already returned to their chores.

Mitch eyed me with concern. "Strange, for sure. What's even stranger is the way Morty was acting, don't you think?"

"I agree. I'll have to take him to the vet first thing in the morning."

"I don't think what ails him can be cured by a doctor."

"What do you mean?"

"I think he's doing what he always does when we're working a case."

My eyes widened. "He's trying to tell us something."

"Exactly." Mitch rubbed his whiskered jaw. "The question is, what?"

BY MONDAY EVENING WE WERE BACK HOME, WITH Vicky's furnace making the place nice and toasty, and a refrigerator full of food. Morty had reappeared, of course, acting perfectly fine. Neither one of us could figure out his clues, so we'd decided to go over what we had so far.

Mitch bit into the roast I'd made, and chewed for far longer than should be necessary. He stabbed a carrot and potato next, and I could hear crunching. They were supposed to be cooked. There shouldn't be crunching. My shoulders wilted, but he just smiled and didn't utter a single complaint. He gave up, set down his fork, and studied his notes, even though I knew he was still hungry. I could hear my own stomach growling, so I grabbed the leftovers Great-Grandma Tootsie had packed for us in a picnic basket. He opened his mouth to say something, but I held up my hand.

"I'm no martyr. What I am is starving. And for the record, I love you for not complaining."

"And I love you for trying," he said softly, then rubbed his hands together and focused. "Okay, so let's put our heads together and see where we're at." Mitch's phone buzzed. He checked the message and rubbed his temples. "Great. Captain Walker wants a progress report. The mayor wants this case closed ASAP. The winter carnival is coming up, and an ongoing murder investigation isn't exactly going to draw the kind of crowd he needs."

"Divinity counts on the carnival for a big source of its revenue, so I get it, but I'm not about to overlook something and risk Cole taking the rap for this."

"I agree." Mitch looked thoughtful for a moment, then he scooped up his notes and added them to the picnic basket with the rest of Grandma Tootsie's goodies.

"What are you doing?"

"Bringing reinforcements."

I groaned, eying the basket with longing. I had planned on dinner in bed, but something told me we weren't going to be eating this for dinner anytime soon. "We're going to butter him up with this food, aren't we?"

"It certainly can't hurt." He looked at me with sympathy. "I feel your pain, Tink. Don't worry. We'll order pizza when we get back. Deal?"

"Just so you know, we're getting the raw end of the deal, but okay."

Ten minutes later, we sat in Captain Walker's office, waiting patiently.

"I think Granny Gert just might have some competition with Great-Grandma Tootsie's cooking." He wiped his mouth with a napkin and moaned as if in heaven.

"Oh, man, those are fighting words, my friend." Mitch pointed at the captain. "Better not let Granny Gert hear you say that."

"Roger that." The captain laughed. "So now that I've eaten, care to fill me in?"

I held out a plate of cookies from Granny Gert and knew I didn't have to say a word.

"Things must be bad if you're pulling out the ace."

The captain snatched the plate and took a seat behind his desk.

"Not bad, just not great for Cole's sake." I sat in the chair beside Mitch. "We still have hope that one of our leads will pan out, but we need more time."

Captain Walker rubbed a hand over his bald head and winced. "That's the problem. I'm not sure how much time I can give you."

"We're just asking for you to hear us out first," Mitch said.

"Done."

My clever detective read from his notes. "So we all know Gunther Corp was found shot to death outside the community center. The last person to see him was Cole West moments earlier when he was heard arguing with Gunther. Cole went for a drive to clear his head, but has no one to corroborate his story. Cole has a concealed-carry license from when he was a correctional officer, and he owns the same caliber of gun used to kill Gunther. Cole's gun is missing. He claims it must have been stolen, yet his house doesn't look broken into, and nothing else was taken. No one can imagine Cole could be capable of murder, yet everyone knows he would do anything to protect his family. It's possible someone is trying to set Cole up. We just have to figure out who and why."

"Agreed," the captain responded while nodding. "Any leads?"

"Well, we did discover Cole wasn't always the most upstanding citizen," I chimed in, reading from my own notes. "He started out in Stillwater as a correctional officer when Gunther was an inmate there. After Gunther got out, Cole got sucked into the Rebel Riders gang. When he saw the length Gunther was willing to go to get what he wanted, Cole got out. He met and married his first wife, Faith Winslow, and moved to Divinity, where he became a carpenter. After Faith died, Cole returned to Stillwater, and Gunther tried to lure him back in. When Cole saw how Gunther was pressuring business owners to give him money for his protection, Cole tried to stop him, and Gunther got badly burned in a fire. Gunther's had it out for Cole ever since."

"I didn't know all that." Captain Walker frowned.

"Not many people do. Cole doesn't like to talk about his past and has worked hard to change his ways and become a respectable, contributing member of the community," I said. "When Gunther came to Divinity, he started harassing Gary at his hardware store, but Cole intervened the best he could. Gary had to know there was only so much Cole could do to stop Gunther, and Gary wasn't about to lose his business. He's put everything he has into making it successful. Gary's a fixer. He helps everyone in town. Maybe he tried to fix the situation, before Divinity became another Stillwater, by taking out Gunther. Gary also has a pistol permit and is a member of the gun club. He would know what kind of gun Cole carries. I can't picture Gary purposely trying to set Cole up, but if he killed Gunther out of desperation, he might have panicked and put the blame on Cole. He witnessed firsthand the animosity between them when they fought in his shop."

"I hope for all our sakes the killer isn't either of them." The captain shook his head. "It would be a shame for Divinity to lose either of these good men."

"Gunther only came to Divinity because IA is investigating the police department in Stillwater," Mitch added. "Too many crimes were overlooked, so they think someone on the inside was turning a blind eye for a cut of the profits. My buddy, Detective Juan Torres, says Officer Adam Burrows covers the East side of Stillwater where the Rebel Riders hang out. If Adam cut Gunther off, then it only makes sense Gunther would be looking for a new turf not far away. But if Gunther got caught, he wasn't about to go down alone. He would rat out Adam in a heartbeat, so maybe Adam followed Gunther to Divinity to get rid of the threat and then pin his murder on someone else, like Cole. Adam called in sick the day of the murder."

"And don't forget we have Gunther's second-in-command, Ray Simone," I added. "I guess it's no secret that Ray wanted Gunther's title as the leader of the Rebel Riders. Gunther treated Ray like crap, and the whole gang didn't like the chances Gunther was taking. He'd become a loose cannon at the end, so maybe Ray took Gunther out. He came to Divinity with Gunther, probably staking out the town, but he easily could have killed him and tried to frame Cole. The rest of the gang would never know, and Ray would logically become their new leader. No one in Divinity saw Ray after Gunther died, and Chuck Webb said he had already checked out when we went to see him at the Divinity Hotel."

"We went to talk to both Ray and Adam in Stillwater yesterday," Mitch stated, "but we didn't have any luck finding them before we ran off the road." His gaze shot to mine before adding, "The damned weather was fierce to drive in."

Yes, and gunning the car in those conditions hadn't been the smartest thing Mitch had ever done. I didn't say a word because I didn't want to talk about the issue between us any more than he did.

"The first tow truck driver's name was Ralph Peters —a giant of a man who seemed harmless enough until we mentioned Gunther Corp," Mitch went on. "It was like he became a different person. Rage filled him, and he let it slip that his wife had been having an affair with Gunther before he died. Of course, he blames Gunther for brainwashing and seducing her. He definitely seemed like he had a side to his personality that could easily commit murder if provoked. We said as much, and he left us there before we could question him further."

We didn't say as much, I wanted to point out. Mitch did. Again, not another smart move, but I couldn't really blame my detective for being off his game after the bomb I had dropped on him.

"Okay, I'll try to stall the mayor as much as I can, but you two need to get to work and find me some answers. Find out if Burrows or Simone have alibis. They definitely have motive. And talk to Gary. He also has motive, but I sure do hope he has an alibi. And someone needs to find out just how unstable Peters is, and if his wife's in any danger. Maybe give Detective Torres a heads-up, since that's his jurisdiction, but if he links either Ralph or his wife to Corp's death, then all bets are off and I want him. Got it?"

"Yes, sir." Mitch nodded once. "We'll do the best we can."

"Do better than that. There's two of you." The captain met eyes with each of us, letting us know, in no uncertain terms, his hands were tied, and the pressure to close this case quickly was on. "Make the most out of the time you have left. Understood?"

"You can't mean—" Mitch started to speak with a tone I knew well.

"Divide and conquer," I interrupted, already standing as I ignored Mitch's frown. He barely agreed to let me be a consultant, but at least he could keep an eye on me that way. He hated when I went rogue and worked on my own, but this time he didn't have a choice. This time I was following orders. "We're on it, Captain."

"Good. Then what are you waiting for?"

8

B y mid-morning on Tuesday, I pulled into the parking lot of Gary's Hardware. He'd missed his weekly horoscope reading, so I'd decided to chase him down. Normally I would just phone and reschedule, but like the Captain said, we were running out of time.

As I'd suspected, Mitch hadn't been happy about me venturing off on my own. I was only allowed to talk to the least threatening of our suspects, and I wasn't to put myself in dangerous situations. Simply question people like Gary, ask around town, poke into some public records, etc. I wasn't a cop, hadn't been trained, and didn't own a gun. I knew that.

But I also wasn't stupid.

I had good instincts that had led to several convictions in the past. Okay, so they had also led to some scary situations, but that couldn't be helped. I promised Captain Walker that I had learned my lesson. I was more careful now, because I had more to lose. Namely my stubborn knucklehead of a fiancé and a chance at a family of my own.

Mitch had headed for Stillwater to talk to Torres about Peters, and to look for Burrows and Simone once more. At least today was a nice day—bright sunshine with no wind and freshly fallen, sparkling white snow that glittered like diamonds.

Grabbing my oversized tote bag, I made my way inside the store. Gary was behind the counter talking to a customer, so I wandered the aisles. Voices from the next row over carried to me. I recognized the voice of Cole's secretary, Cathy Grossman.

"Are you okay?" Cathy said. "You don't look so good."

"Gee, thanks," a familiar voice grunted.

"I didn't mean it that way. I'm just really worried about you."

"I'll manage," the voice responded after a lengthy pause. "The pain will eventually pass. It always does."

I peeked through the shelves and saw Cole's buddy Zack Kruger. He rubbed the end of his amputated arm and shifted from foot to foot.

"You shouldn't have to go through this. You've been through enough." She tucked her bright red hair behind her ears and her soft green eyes gazed at him adoringly.

His gaze met hers and held. "So have you."

She was the first to look away, her pale skin flushing and making the spattering of freckles stand out. "You still having nightmares?"

He shrugged. "How do you know about that?"

She winced sympathetically. "Cole told me. He's worried about you, too."

"He's the one we should all be worried about. I'll get through this. He might not. I'm not the one with a wife pregnant with twins. He's the one who has been through a lot after losing Faith. I can't let him lose Jo and the twins too."

"What are you going to do?"

"I don't know. There has to be some way to help."

Guilt stabbed through me over avoiding Jo and Cole lately. I justified it by saying they had each other to lean on, and I had a job to do if we were ever going to clear Cole's name. The truth was I was terrified that wouldn't happen. Jo was my best friend. I couldn't look her in the eye and pretend like everything was going to be okay. What if it wasn't?

I bumped into the shelf and knocked over a hammer, sending it crashing to the floor with a loud bang.

Zack whirled around in a crouched position, whipping his good arm up as if to protect himself. Cathy reached for his arm to steady him, but he stepped back, evading her touch. She dropped her hand and looked down at the floor.

I rushed around the shelves until I stood beside them in their aisle. "I am so sorry. Clumsy me is always knocking things over. I hope I didn't cause either of you any harm."

He straightened, letting his muscles relax. He looked tired. "No worries, Miss Meadows. I'm fine. Gotta run now. Good seeing you again." He quickly left the store. As quickly as one could with a limp.

"He's so stubborn." Cathy stared after him with a look of longing on her face. "Too proud to ever ask for help, even though he clearly needs it."

"I'm sure Doc Wilcox would clear his schedule for a local hero."

Cathy's sad gaze met mine. "That's not the kind of doctor he needs, I'm afraid."

"Oh," I said quietly. "Have you known him long?"

Her face lit up with genuine pleasure. "I have known Zackery Kruger since he and Miles and Cole first moved to Divinity and worked together in construction. I got a job as Cole's secretary and never left.

They were really something to behold when they were together. Always raising a ruckus with plenty of laughter thrown in. The Three Musketeers." Her smiled faded. "But after Faith died, everything changed."

"What happened?" I sensed she needed someone to listen to her.

"Miles left to lick his wounds in private, and Zack joined the service because he was angry, but I stayed to be there for Cole." She smiled at me sadly. "There was nothing else for me to do. Zack didn't only leave Divinity, he left me. We had just started seeing each other, but I guess that wasn't enough to make him stay. He might have left angry, but he came back broken, and I have no idea how to fix him."

"I'm so sorry, Cathy." I squeezed her hand.

"It's okay. I'm a strong woman. Besides how can I be mad at him? He's already been through so much."

"Give him time. Maybe things will change."

"Maybe." She lifted a shoulder, not looking very hopeful. "Well, I better get these supplies back to Cole before he starts worrying about that, too." She headed up front to pay Gary, and I made a vow right then and there not to be a coward anymore.

There were people in the world who had gone through far worse than me. No more avoiding Jo and Cole. They needed to know there was a ticking clock. They needed to know that we didn't have much to go on. They needed to know the truth.

But not before I had done everything in my power to change the outcome.

"HI, GARY, REMEMBER ME?" I SMILED UP AT HIM.

He looked at me with a guilty expression on his face. "I meant to call," was all he said.

"And I meant to take my vitamins this morning, but I forgot. Life happens. I get that, but it's not too late." I glanced at the clock. "Why, look at that. I do believe it's your lunch hour. Doesn't Billy Rowe have half days in school this year since he's a senior? I seem to remember my mother mentioning what a good job he did when he waited on her just the other day, right around this time. Can't he cover for you while I give you a reading?"

"Oh, that's all right. I wouldn't have time to get over to your place and back, and he's still new. I really don't want to leave him alone."

"No worries." I patted my tote bag. "I brought my office to you. I would feel terrible if you missed a reading, since you already paid me for the entire month."

Billy walked in right then and waved to Gary, then stored his things in the back room and took his place behind the counter. "I'm here, boss. I got you covered."

"Great, Billy." Gary's smile was a bit stiff and full of resignation. "That's just great." His shoulders drooped a little with weariness as he led the way into his back room.

Gary loved his readings. He lived to hear what his horoscope had to say. That was why it was a little confusing and a whole lot alarming for him to be hesitant in having me read his sign today. Unless he was afraid of what I would discover. I took a deep breath and reminded myself this was Gary we were talking about. A nice, respectable man whom I had known for a year now. Then again, he was also a person of interest in a murder investigation. If I had learned anything over the past year, it was that appearances could be deceiving and anything was possible.

Gary shut the door behind us and gestured for me to take a seat at the break room table. "It's not exactly your sanctuary, but it will have to do," he muttered, clearly not acting like he was into this reading at all.

I sat across from him and pulled out my horoscope charts. "Is everything okay, Gary? You're usually so excited for your weekly readings, yet you missed today and didn't call to reschedule."

Gary's tight, curly brown hair and mustache looked trimmed and neat. He was tall and skinny, with a slight limp, but still sat up straight and strong. He liked to help people and didn't let excuses get in the way of that, but right now, behind closed doors, he finally let his guard down. His shoulders slumped ever so slightly, but I noticed. "It's been a rough week," was all he said.

"Well, then, let's see if we can find out why." I smiled encouragingly as I spread my charts out before me to study them. I genuinely liked Gary. I was with the captain. I hoped like heck that he was innocent.

Gary was an air sign. He loved to communicate and form relationships with other people. Born a thinker, he was analytical, communicative, and intellectual. He loved social gatherings, good books, and philosophical discussions. If asked, he readily gave advice, but at times he could be superficial. All in all, he was a great guy, which made this all the more difficult.

As an Aquarius, he was a progressive, original, independent humanitarian. The problem was, he often ran from expressing himself emotionally. That was why he had issues with finding someone to share his life with. The fact that he was temperamental, sometimes aloof, and often uncompromising didn't help.

I did, however, point out that he liked to help others and fight for their causes. He was fun to be around, could definitely hold an intellectual conversation, and was a great listener. He didn't like to be limited, abhorred broken promises, avoided people who disagreed with him, dull and boring situations, and hated being lonely. His kind had a reputation for being cold and insensitive, but he really wasn't. It was just his defense mechanism against premature intimacy.

Gary needed to learn to trust others before he could express his emotions in a healthy way. Because once he did, he would be loyal and committed. He would consider his partner an equal and never try to possess them, sacrificing everything for their happiness. Gary often lived inside his own mind. That was why he came to me each week. He needed someone to talk to about the progressive thoughts he had. I was the next best thing to a therapist for him.

"Well, anything?" he asked anxiously.

"Actually, yes. This is an excellent time of year for you to form new relationships and build new social contacts. Let's start with your career."

"Okay." His forehead puckered, and I could tell he wanted to know what I had to say, but he was somehow afraid as well.

"Your argumentative nature may not help matters in your career. There is a fine balance between aggression and harmony in dealing with others. You'd do well to remember that. I know you want to help people in this town, but you can't always fix everything, Gary."

"I know." He looked down at his hands as he interlocked his fingers and rotated his thumbs.

"I know you have big dreams when it comes to expanding your business. You've done such a great job with this place. I'm sure you'll be successful, but look for loyalty when making new relationships and friendships. It's time, Gary. You need to change some outdated ideas and be open to new creativity in your work."

He looked up at me and his eyes widened as if I'd touched on something. "So, you think I should say 'yes'?"

Oh, boy. "That depends on what you're saying 'yes' to." I had to be careful about getting carried away when advising certain people. Gary lived by his readings. He was obviously going through something, and the last thing I wanted to do was steer him in the wrong direction. "Are you referring to business or pleasure?"

"Both, maybe."

"Well, I do see you starting a new venture. You'll need to get the cooperation and help from others." I frowned. "But I also see your expenses overshooting and upsetting your budget. Be careful that your expenses for personal luxuries doesn't take over. I think everything will stabilize in time. Work out a financial plan to balance your earnings and expenses, and you will be fine."

He let out a huge breath of air. "That's good to hear."

I looked at him with concern. "This venture will require energy and stamina if you don't want to suffer a nervous breakdown. You can't just work hard. You need to mix relaxation in as well, to maintain a healthy disposition. I recommend meditation. I hear it works wonders."

He dropped his gaze to the table and his face flushed.

"I take it that's the pleasure part of the complicated mix?"

Finally, his gaze met mine. "Cindy Malone down at the spa has an amazing pair of hands."

This time I blushed.

"I mean she gives a great relaxing massage." His face flamed red. "She also teaches meditation. My parents weren't on board with my plans, so I sought her out through a friend's recommendation and she helped me to relax. I somehow found myself opening up to her, which *so* isn't like me, and suddenly she offers to invest. I backed off, of course. It was a bit too much, too soon, if you know what I mean. But I can't stop thinking about her, and I can't help wondering if I made a mistake. She's witty and clever and funny." His tender smile said it all. "And she's smarter than anyone I've ever met."

"She sounds perfect." I squeezed his hand. "Isn't she everything you've ever been looking for?"

"Yes, and that terrifies me."

"Being engaged to Mitch terrifies me, but when you meet *The One* you just know it. I say go for it, on one condition."

He looked at me curiously. "What's that?"

"Where were you the afternoon Gunther Corp was murdered?"

He blinked. "Pardon me?"

"I hate to say this, but I have to. Gunther threatened your business and might have been ready to threaten other businesses in Divinity if someone didn't stop him. You like to fix things, and you're a member of the gun club. Then you cancel our appointment and act all skittish. So as much as I hate to do this, I repeat... where were you the afternoon Gunther Corp was murdered?"

He stared at me for a long moment. "I get why you asked, and I don't blame you. You're only doing your job. Gunther did infuriate me, and if he had come back, I honestly don't know what I would have done to protect my town. I don't condone murder, but I am glad that decision is out of my hands now. I was at Cindy's place, getting a massage. That's the same day she made me the offer to invest in my business. And that is why I have been so freaked out. You can ask her. I'm sure she'll verify my alibi."

I let out a huge sigh of relief. "I believe you, Gary. And for the record, don't be afraid to let her in. I don't know Cindy, but she sounds like a fantastic person. Exactly what you need, if you ask me. And if she's smart like you say, then she will make a great business partner. You can't go wrong, so I say go for it."

"You think so?" he asked, looking hopeful.

I donned my best fortune-teller face as I responded with utmost conviction, "I *know* so."

9

"I'm sorry. We shouldn't have been avoiding you guys," I said to Jo and Cole while sitting at the bar in Smokey Jo's Tavern. It was a slow night in the small town of Divinity, so no chance of being over-heard and sending the ever-churning rumor mill into overdrive.

"*We* haven't been doing anything. *You* have," Mitch responded from beside me. "Some of us have been working."

My jaw unhinged, and I gaped at him. "Seriously? You're really going to throw me under the bus like that, Detective? Last I checked, you haven't been knocking on their door any more than I have."

"Because I didn't have any answers for them. I'm all about the facts, Tink. No sense wasting anyone's time until I have some."

"You're all about something, Grumpy Pants, and facts have nothing to do with it. Avoidance with a cap-ital A is more like it." And suddenly we weren't talking about the case anymore.

Cole popped open a longneck and handed it to Mitch. "It's on the house. Why don't you come with me and fill me in on those facts, buddy?"

"Probably a good idea," Mitch grumbled as he stood and followed Cole a little too quickly.

"I've got the snacks," Sean added just as hastily.

"Men," Jo said, handing me a beer.

"Amen," Zoe seconded, as she poured herself a glass of wine.

"Speaking of men, how's everything going between you two?" Jo sipped her milk.

"Tense, because we're both still avoiding our own issues and focusing on the bigger issue of clearing Cole's name. You know Mitch, he can't stand the fact that Captain Walker wants me on the case as well."

"He's just worried," Zoe said.

"We both are," I admitted, "and not just about our relationship." My gaze met Jo's. "We're running out of time. The mayor wants this case resolved ASAP with the Winterfest coming up, yet none of our leads are panning out."

"They will." Jo rubbed her massive stomach.

I eyed her with curiosity and a bit of wariness. "You sound so sure and confident. How is that possible?"

"Mother's intuition," she responded immediately. "Don't ask me how I know, I just do. My babies and I need our Sasquatch. The universe wouldn't take that away from us. That's all there is to it."

Zoe and I eyed each other with concern. I hoped Jo was right, because if we couldn't clear Cole's name, I wasn't sure she could handle the reality of what her life would become as a single mother of twins, a fur baby mommy of a Great Dane puppy, and a business owner. She'd be having a nervous breakdown of the Amazonian kind.

As if reading our thoughts, Cole, Mitch, and Sean joined us with grim looks on their faces.

"What's wrong, babe, you look pale?" Jo asked Cole.

"Nothing for you to worry about. Probably something I ate." He tried for a smile.

"I was just filling him in on where we're at in the case," Mitch said in full detective mode, except now was not the time for a reality check.

"So, did you hear the news?" Sean chimed in as if sensing the vibe that a certain pregnant woman was fragile right now, unlike a clueless Detective Stone.

Zoe's shoulders wilted as if in relief, and she shot her boyfriend a grateful glance. Pasting on a dramatic expression, she faced me. "The mayor moved up the date for Winterfest."

I stifled a gasp. "That's a huge event. It takes so much planning; the committee must be freaking out." I shook my head.

"Oh, they're not the only ones freaking out." Jo chuckled.

"What do you mean?" I felt my forehead pucker.

"Well, Chuck Webb has a business to run as well, and he already booked rooms during the new dates."

"But he's the only hotel in town," I replied.

"Not the *only* one," Jo said meaningfully.

"Oh, Lord have mercy, you mean my mother?" I sputtered. "The inn isn't nearly ready to be open that soon. My mother must be going insane."

"That's an understatement." Cole grunted.

"Let's just say they're going to need *divine inspiration* for the inn to be ready on time." Sean grimaced.

"As if we didn't have enough to worry about right now."

"I THOUGHT YOU MIGHT BE HUNGRY," I SAID LATER THAT night, and carried a pizza out to the garage—the one area Morty would allow Mitch to put his stamp on.

I had a feeling my detective was avoiding me again, though he would deny it if I said anything. He looked up from the notes he'd spread out on the pool table and tried for a smile, but the crease in the middle of his forehead was too deep to fade completely.

"Thanks." He straightened and rubbed the back of his neck with his big hand.

My heart melted. No matter what we were going through personally, I knew he was working so hard to clear his best friend's name. His loyalty and protective nature for those he cared about were some of the things I loved the most about him.

"I know Captain told us to divide and conquer, but that doesn't mean we're not a team anymore," I said softly. "I told you about Gary's reading, yet you never did tell me what you found out from Torres. Maybe I can help."

"I'm sorry. We've hardly spent more than a couple minutes together lately, and we ran out of time." He sat down and picked up a slice of pizza, taking a bite and closing his eyes for a moment to chew.

"It's okay." I walked around him to rub his shoulders and massage his neck, giving him the time he needed to gather his thoughts. He leaned his head back against me and groaned in sheer bliss, and I couldn't resist bending down to kiss the top of his head. "I'm here now."

He reached up and squeezed my hand. "I know, and I love you."

"I love you too." Our love wasn't in question. Whether it would be enough to withstand our differences on having a baby remained to be seen. But I missed him and right now I needed to feel his strength.

He pulled me around to the front of him and down onto his lap. Wrapping his arms around me, he started talking. "I didn't have any luck finding Adam or Ray, but I did learn some interesting facts from Torres. Internal Affairs didn't have enough evidence on Burrows to do anything about his alleged shady dealings with the biker gang, so they had to clear him."

"Then why can't you find him?"

"He took a leave of absence from the emotional stress of being wrongly accused, and is recuperating out of town."

"Where?"

"No one knows."

I snuggled deeper into his arms and mumbled against his chest, "Do you think he's innocent?"

Mitch ran his palms slowly up and down my back, making it hard to focus on what he was saying. "Not a chance. Torres has great instincts. If he doesn't believe him, then that's good enough for me."

"What are we going to do about it?"

He hesitated over the word *we* for a moment, then responded with heavy resignation in his voice, "Dig deeper."

"Tomorrow." I flattened my palms against his chest, feeling his heartbeat quicken.

"What about it?"

"Let's start tomorrow. Tonight, we need to recharge our batteries." I peeked up and drank in the site of him. "I miss you, Grumpy Pants."

"Me, too, Tink." His gaze dropped to my mouth. "Me, too," he repeated with a husky tone to his deep voice before lowering his lips to mine and showing me just how much.

THE NEXT DAY I WALKED DOWN MAIN STREET TOWARD A small deli that carried gourmet cheese, meats, and delicacies. My mother was a fancy, Grey Poupon type of woman, while I was more of a plain Jane, basic mustard sort of girl. Her picky self would never shop at Gretta's Mini Mart for her specialty items. While I normally stuck with the basics, I wanted to give my mother a little pick-me-up. Besides, I gave Gretta plenty of business, and this shop was another local mom-and-pop store. I was all about supporting Divinity's local businesses.

Winterfest was fast approaching. The streets were evident of that. Sparkly snowflakes hung from the old-fashioned light posts, while several fake snowmen were animatedly decorated and staggered alongside the benches. Flyers with all the upcoming events were stapled to the telephone poles, and various sales were advertised in storefront windows. Winterfest was one of our biggest carnivals, taking over most of the town. Streets shut down for the many outdoor activities for young and old. Craft tents were set up for locals to sell their wares. My favorite was skating on the pond, and I couldn't wait to do it as a couple with Mitch. Knowing my man these days, he would be anticipating the chili cook-off which wrapped up the festival at the end of the week.

The pressure to close this case in a hurry trickled down from the mayor to Chief Spencer to Captain Walker and inevitably to Mitch and me. I sometimes wondered if they even cared who went to jail, as long as someone did. Well, I refused to let that happen. As two of our most well-respected, contributing members of the community, Jo and Cole deserved more than that from all of us.

With Winterfest came an increase in tourist activity and vendors from all over, which only complicated matters when it came to investigating a crime of any kind. With so many new faces milling about, it was hard to keep track of suspects and motives and new leads. It was only going to get worse as the festival grew closer.

After popping into A Cut Above and ordering a fancy spread for my mother, I stepped outside to head over to Smokey Jo's to meet up with Jo and Zoe. We were trying to take Jo's mind off her worries, and head out to the inn to help my mother get ready to open. It started to snow, so I tightened my coat and squinted to keep the flakes from blurring my vision. I picked up the pace and held my treasured goods tighter. My toe caught on a piece of ice and off I went, slipping and sliding, until finally falling on my backside. I hit my head and saw stars as pain rocketed through my brain, but I managed to save the food.

Rubbing my head until the throbbing subsided, I gingerly sat up, bracing myself against the biting chill in the air. I stared straight ahead and sucked in a breath. Wait a minute. I blinked to clear my vision, thinking I must have a concussion. I couldn't have seen what I thought I did, could I? I searched the entire area, but the couple was gone. I could have sworn I just saw Ray Simone and Kristen Peters, but that didn't make any sense. What on earth were they doing in Divinity, and more importantly...

Why were they together?

Gingerly hoisting myself to my feet, I trudged through the slushy snow until I reached Smokey Jo's, only to stop short. What on earth was happening today? Detective Fuller was standing on the street, inspecting the broken window.

I came to a stop by Jo and Zoe. "Are you guys okay?"

"We're both fine." Jo waved away my concern and focused on what Fuller was saying to her, her expression growing angrier with every word.

"What happened?" I asked Zoe.

"Someone had the gall to break into Smokey Jo's." Zoe shook her head. "I pity the fool when Jo finds out who it is."

"No kidding. Even pregnant, Joanne Burnham West is a force to be reckoned with." I scanned the area and peeked inside. "Did they take anything?"

"That's the funny thing. They didn't steal anything —just smashed the front window and some glasses. Almost as if they wanted to make a statement. I would guess it was the Rebel Riders, but how can that be? Gunther's dead."

"His second-in-command, Ray Simone, isn't. I thought I was seeing things earlier. When I came out of the deli, I could have sworn I saw Ray with Ralph Peter's wife, Kristen, based on the pictures I've seen from our research."

"Do you honestly think he would return to Divinity and finish what they started, when he could be a suspect in his former boss's murder?"

"From what I gather, he's pretty ballsy. I wouldn't put anything past him. I just can't figure out why Kristen Peters was with him."

"I have no clue, but you might want to start with this guy." Zoe pointed to a middle-aged man with blonde hair and a mustache. "He's one of the craft vendors who just arrived in town for the festival, and he's been setting up his stand right outside of Smokey Jo's all morning. Maybe he saw something."

"Good idea." I walked over to the curb and stepped under the tent he'd rigged up. "Excuse me." I smiled politely and held out my hand. "My name is Sunshine Meadows."

The man blinked pale blue eyes in surprise, but quickly smiled in return. "I'm Wayne Emerson. It's nice to meet you, Ms. Meadows."

"Please, call me Sunny. Welcome to Divinity."

"Why, thank you, Sunny." He glanced at the gray sky full of fat flakes. "Hopefully the weather turns around for the festival."

"Oh, believe me, snow will only add to Winterfest."

He chuckled. "That's true. Don't know what I was thinking."

"Is this your first time here? I don't remember seeing you last year."

"It sure is. I just started woodworking and discovered I have a knack for it, so I thought it would be worth trying to sell some of my pieces."

He hadn't unpacked any products yet so I couldn't see the quality, but he sounded pretty confident. "Well, good luck to you. I'm sure you'll do great."

"Thank you. I sure hope so." He turned around to start working on his tent again.

"Wayne?"

He kept pulling the tarp down with his back to me.

"Hey, Wayne?" I repeated. "Do you mind if I ask you a question."

"Oh, I'm sorry." He said after turning around and seeing me still standing there. "I didn't realize you were talking to me. What did you ask?"

"I was just wondering if you happened to see anything last night or this morning? I'm sure you've heard by now that someone broke into my friend's bar and did a fair amount of damage."

He rubbed his jaw and stared off in concentration. "It's a downright shame what happened to her place of business. Makes me worry it might happen to some of us vendors. I almost didn't come to Divinity after I heard about the recent murder, but I figured if Winterfest was still on, then everything must be okay." He glanced at Smokey Jo's with concern. "Maybe I was wrong."

"I'm sure everything will be fine. Do you remember seeing anything at all that seemed out of place or suspicious?"

"Can't say that I do. Sorry, Sunny. I really wish I could help."

"It's okay, Wayne. I appreciate you taking the time to talk with me. If you think of anything at all, you can reach me here." I handed him my business card. "I consult for the Divinity Police Department on the side."

He stared at the card for a moment, then nodded once as his gaze met mine. "Will do."

I started to walk back over to Jo and Zoe when Wayne's words made me freeze.

"Hey, Sunny, I just thought of something that did seem a little off."

I turned around to face him expectantly.

"There was this bear of a man this morning. Looked like a bald-headed giant with a beard longer than I've ever seen. Said he was looking for his wife and showed me a picture. She was a pretty thing. Can't imagine what she sees in him, but that's neither here nor there. It was probably nothing, he was just acting antsy and strange is all."

"Thank you. That actually helps more than you know." Looked like Ray and Kristen weren't the only suspects who'd returned to Divinity...

Ralph Peters was here as well.

10

I raised my hand to knock on the door to my parents' inn, but it swung open before I could.

"Where have you been, young lady?" my mother asked, her face puckered into a sour expression.

"Working, but I'm here now." I bit back what I really wanted to say and handed her the basket of deli goods I'd bought.

"Who has time to eat with so much left to do?" She took the basket from me, barely glancing inside. "Well, get on in here. Better late than never I guess."

My mother had never been the soft, supportive, comforting type. I knew that she loved me, and we'd come to a truce of sorts, but I still longed for things to be different at times. Her whole face brightened when she spotted Zoe and Jo, then lingered wistfully on Jo's baby belly. A little piece of my heart squeezed tight in envy. I knew she didn't mean anything by it, but seeing her so affectionate with them stung. I knew she wanted to be a grandmother. As her only child, the pressure was on me. Little did she know, for once we were on the same page. I just didn't know if my fiancé was.

"There's my darling daughter," came a booming voice from behind me. I spun around and my father wrapped me in a bear hug, making me feel ten again. He still wasn't a true believer in my fortune-telling abilities, but at least he accepted me for who I was now. He used to push me to do something more with my life, but he was getting soft now that he was retired and I was engaged. He probably figured I had Mitch to take care of me for the rest of our lives, and I didn't have the heart to tell him that might not be the case anymore.

"Good to see you, girl. I was just on my way out to join Harry. Your mother has us all running around in circles with to-do lists." He dramatically rolled his eyes, my mother none the wiser as she fussed over Jo while she filled her in on the break-in. "People will sleep just as well here if the grounds aren't in perfect shape. Harry and I can only work so fast. We have our own lists." He patted his chest proudly. "We're in charge of the ice fishing contest for Winterfest."

"That's great, Dad. I'm sure you guys will do a wonderful job."

"Thanks for the vote of confidence, kiddo." He winked and headed for the door the second my mother spotted him lollygagging.

She raised a brow at me as if it were somehow my fault. Hoisting her chin a notch, she marched over to me with Jo and Zoe following closely behind. "Mitch, Sean, Cole, and his friends all finished painting for me just about an hour ago, so be careful. The walls might still be wet."

"It looks great, Mom," I said, and meant it.

My mother had always had impeccable tastes. Rich, neutral earth tones with updated molding and accents adorned the walls. The hardwood floors had been refurbished, and new pieces of furniture had replaced the old, outdated ones. Frank had installed new heating and cooling units, while Sally made everything sparkle. Thank the Lord it was winter, because who knew what shape the yard was in with Harry and my dad in charge, but something smelled great coming from the kitchen.

"Thank you, I appreciate that. It sure hasn't been easy," she admitted in a rare moment of vulnerability, then she squared her shoulders and the moment was gone. "We'd better get this basket in the refrigerator." She hesitated a moment before her eyes met mine. "Thank you, darling. I didn't realize what you handed me earlier. It looks divine."

It shouldn't matter what I had handed her to prompt a thank you, but hey, I would take what I could get. And that was as close to an apology as I would ever expect to hear from her. "You're welcome."

She nodded once, then led the way.

We followed my mother into the kitchen, and I had to bite back a chuckle. The Tasty Trio was hard at work. Great-Grandma Tootsie was dressed in her usual polyester, with a checkered apron tied around her waist, cooking up a storm from memory, no recipe book in sight. She hummed a lively tune as she worked, then straightened as much as she could, as she held a wooden spoon and directed the kitchen like a maestro directs his symphony. Fiona was dressed in the latest fashion as she baked pies with perfectly manicured nails, and then there was Granny Gert, with her snow-white hair and flour sack aprons, baking cookies.

"Boys oh day, I think we have some winners, ladies." Toots clapped her hands.

"I think you're right," Fiona replied. "You can't go

wrong with pie, and my lemon meringue is the best in the county."

"Well, land sakes, I *know* she's right," Granny twittered. "Why, these here cookies are some of the best I've baked in a long time, and my Special K bars are show-stoppers."

"Now listen here, you two. You're both terrific bakers, and this isn't a bakeoff. You're both winners in my book, and that's something to celebrate. At my age, I'll take any reason to celebrate. It's time for a rye and ginger, if I do say so myself."

"If those recipes taste as good as they smell, I'll join you," my mother said, surprising me. She and Granny Gert had never been that close, but she'd seemed to have taken a shine to Great-Grandma Tootsie. I could relate, as I was much closer to my grandmother than my own mother. "I don't know what I would have done if you hadn't come along, Toots." My mother gave the elderly woman a quick hug.

"Oh, go on with you now. You all would have done just fine without me, but I sure am glad to be needed for a change. I'm happy you like the smells, but the real test will be on the fellows sitting in the dining room." She clapped her hands twice. "Chop chop, girls. Lend a hand and let's serve those boys out there. They've been working awful hard."

Jo, Zoe, and I, and even my mother hastened to do Toots' bidding, while Fiona, Granny, and Toots brought up the rear. Mitch, Sean, Cole, Miles, and Zack sat at the table, looking hungry and ready to drool. Harry, Frank, and my father came in and joined them. And last but not least, Captain Walker took the seat at the head of the table, while Granny, Fiona, and Toots all rushed over to dote on him. I should be surprised, but I totally wasn't.

"Captain Walker?" I asked. "I didn't expect to see you here."

"I stopped in to see if these fine ladies needed any help."

"And did you help?" I bit back a smile.

"He helped, all right." Mitch chuckled. "He's been their taste tester for the past hour. You'd think he would save some for the rest of us."

Captain Walker puffed up his chest. "Just doing my civic duty and serving my town." Then he gave in and rubbed his full belly.

"Convenient that it's right at lunch time," Mitch pointed out.

"Hey, a man's gotta eat." Captain Walker held up his hands and tried to look innocent, but no one was buying it.

"Well, say now, there's plenty for everyone." Toots scurried around the table, completely in her element taking care of her newfound family.

Everyone ate in silence, other than the occasional moan over how delicious everything was. After we all agreed the menu was a winner, Captain Walker and Mitch went back to work while Sean and Zoe went off to man the bar. Repairs on Smokey Jo's were being done already, but for the most part, the bar was serviceable.

"I'm furious someone would target my business," Jo said. "Why me?"

"It's not just you," Miles chimed in. "I heard Warm Beginnings and Cozy Endings café, and Sam's Bakery got hit also. Sounds like whoever is doing this is going after the town's businesses."

"Doesn't make me feel any better. It makes me even madder. It has to be the Rebel Riders. No one has the right to strong-arm businesses into paying for protection."

"I saw Ray and Kristen in town together this morning. And then I talked to a vendor who said a man matching Ralph Peters' description was in town looking for his wife. No sign of Officer Burrows yet, but there's enough suspicion linked to the other three, I think it's time to find them and question them. At the very least, tail them to make sure no one else's business gets broken into. It can't be a coincidence that they show up in town at the same time that these businesses were hit. I'll talk to Mitch later and see what he thinks."

"Sorry, Jo," Zack said, not quite meeting her eyes. "You shouldn't have to go through any of this."

"No, she shouldn't. This is all my fault." Cole's jaw worked overtime.

"Sometimes life sucks, and there isn't anything we can do about it." Miles stared off in the distance, lost in memories.

"Oh, there's something we can do about it." Cole squeezed Miles' shoulder. "And you can bet I will."

"You won't be doing any such thing, Sasquatch." Jo poked him in the chest and Cole dropped his hand to rub the spot. "I can take care of myself, but you are not going to abandon our babies by talking like that or doing something stupid."

"I agree. Nothing good ever comes from revenge," Zack said quietly, then sniffed and rubbed his nose.

"I'm sure justice will be served in the end," Miles added. "Let the police handle this." He turned to my mother. "Do you need us to do anything else before we leave, Mrs. Meadows?"

"No, thank you, Miles. You all were such a big help

today. I hope you stay with us for free once the regular season opens."

"If I ever need a place to stay, you can count on it." He nodded, then looked at Zack. "I'm headed your way. You need a ride?"

"Sure," Zack replied, without making eye contact as he limped to the door to grab his coat.

"Wait, I packed some left-over chicken soup for that cold of yours." Toots handed the container to Zack, and Zack flinched. Squeezing his eyes closed for a second, he opened them and smiled slightly at her. "Thank you, ma'am." He took the soup, careful not to touch her hand, and my heart broke for him. Cathy was right. He was hurting in more ways than one, and I wasn't sure he would ever heal completely.

Just then Morty appeared from out of nowhere. Everyone except Zack jumped. In fact, he did the most remarkable thing. He picked up Morty, and shockingly, Morty let him. Zack took a moment to cuddle Morty and seemed to visibly relax with him in his arms. He whispered something to my cat who purred and rubbed against him before jumping out of his arms. And then Zack left.

Morty the therapy cat? What next?

THE NEXT MORNING, I KNOCKED ON THE OFFICE DOOR TO West Construction.

"Did you bring the stuff?" Cole asked as he opened the door.

I patted my fringed satchel. "I've got you covered, my friend."

He glanced around and then stepped back and

motioned me inside. "You parked out back, right? Not too many people have a floral-painted VW Bug for a car. If anyone drove by, they'd know you were here, hanging out with a murderer." He closed the door behind me.

"Alleged murderer—in fact, you're only a suspect. It doesn't matter to me if anyone sees me here, Cole. You didn't do anything wrong."

"Tell that to the judge." He grunted.

"I will if I have to, but it won't come to that. I have faith that Mitch and I will clear your name and put the real killer behind bars."

"I really hope so. I can handle whatever happens to me. Hell, I've been through worse, but I can't stomach what losing me would do to Jo and our babies."

"Then let's get to work."

"Do you really think reading my fortune will help?"

"The way I look at it is that it certainly can't hurt."

I followed Cole over to the couch and spread my horoscope charts on the coffee table in front of it. Taking the seat next to him, I studied the charts for a moment. "You're an Earth sign. No wonder Jo loves you. Earth signs are the grounded people who bring the rest of us down to earth."

"What can I say, I try my best." He looked uncomfortable with flattery.

"For the most part you're conservative and realistic, but I've seen first-hand that you can be very emotional, especially when it comes to those you love. You're so practical and loyal and stable, always sticking by your people through hard times. We're all lucky to have you in our lives, Cole. You should know that."

He smiled a little and everything about him relaxed. "I do know that, and thank you. It means a lot."

"Okay, on to your sign. I see you're a Virgo. That doesn't surprise me, since Virgos are loyal, kind, analytical, hardworking, and practical. That sums you up to a T."

"I guess so. Anything bad about being a Virgo?"

"Well, you do have some weaknesses. You can be shy, you tend to worry a lot, you are often overly critical of yourself, and sometimes you're all work and no play."

He looked down with chagrin. "I'm working on that."

"And you like animals, healthy food, books, nature, and cleanliness, while you hate rudeness, asking for help, and being the center of attention."

"Well, that's not all bad."

"No, but just know it's okay to let other people who care about you take charge sometimes."

"I know, and trust me, I am. My fate is in your and Detective Stone's hands."

No pressure, I thought, but sat up straight and reached out to touch his arm. "We're doing our best not to let you down."

Before he could reply, I tightened my grip on his arm as the room before me started to spin. I could vaguely hear him asking me if I was okay, but I couldn't answer. Just like it always did, the world around me narrowed into tunnel vision, and suddenly I was someone else.

My breathing picked up and my pulse started to race. I could feel my palms sweat as I gripped Cole's arm in desperation. I felt like if I let go, my world would crumble around me. I started to shake and felt like I would fall over at any moment. Suddenly pain shot through me.

"Sunny, can you hear me? Are you okay? Please answer me," a deep voice cut through my fog, and I let go.

I blinked and saw Cole watching me with a mixture of fear and helplessness in his eyes. "You cried out like someone was killing you. What the hell was that about?"

Taking several deep, calming breaths, my body became my own again and I could breathe. "I think I was in a nightmare. I couldn't stop shaking, and I felt fear and guilt and pain."

Cole was already nodding. "It has to be the stress I'm going through. I just had a nightmare last night and it really shook me up. I woke up sweating and felt so guilty over what I'm putting my wife and babies through. All because I let my temper get the best of me. You have to help me, Sunny. I'll never be able to live with myself if I go to prison. The thought of Jo handling everything on her own because of my stupidity will kill me. I never should have let Gunther get the best of me. I should have walked away and ignored him and gone home where I belong. Instead, I argued with him and fought him and drove off alone with no one knowing where I was. All of this is my fault."

"You didn't kill him, Cole. You're innocent. I know it doesn't seem like it right now, but justice will prevail. I have to believe and have faith, and so do you."

"I'm trying, Sunny. I really am, but it's hard." He rubbed his forearm where I'd dug my nails in during my vision. No wonder I felt pain in my arm. "I'm sorry about that." I pointed to the marks my nail made over a tattoo of the Three Musketeers.

His lips twisted into a half smile. "I think I can handle a few fingernail marks." His smile faded. "Trust me, I've been through worse."

"Not this time," I responded, and thought, *Not on my watch.*

11

After I left West Construction, I headed straight to Healing Hands. I walked inside and was pleasantly surprised. Soft meditation music filtered through the sound system, relaxing me instantly. The walls were painted a calming pale blue, the waiting room chairs soft and inviting. Lemon and orange water, as well as cucumber water, sat invitingly on a table off to the side, along with warm fingertip towels. A woman with slicked-back gray hair sat behind the desk.

"Hi, my name is Sunshine Meadows and I have an appointment with Cindy."

"Well, hello there, Sunny. I'm Amy, Cindy's office manager." She held out her hand and shook mine. "We've heard all about you from Gary."

"Good things, I hope." I smiled.

Amy grinned. "Only the best. Gary's a big fan of your abilities. I know Cindy has been dying to meet you."

"Sorry I haven't been in before now. Things have been crazy busy lately. I always try to meet the owners of any new businesses that come to town. I mean, we can all use each other's support, right? So, if you or Cindy ever need a reading, you know where to find me."

"You got it. If you want to take a seat, Cindy will be right with you."

I sank into a luxurious chair and couldn't help but moan. It felt like forever since I had taken a moment to relax. I closed my eyes and inhaled deep.

"You *must* be Sunny. You look exactly like Gary described you," came a lyrical voice from somewhere in the room.

My eyes popped open, and my lips tipped up instantly. A petite woman with pink hair, lavender eyes and a beaming smile stood before me with her hand held out, waiting.

"I, um, yes... that's me." I stood and shook her hand. She didn't look like she weighed more than a hundred pounds, and I found myself wondering how she could possibly be strong enough to massage half the big burly men of Divinity. I suddenly realized I was judging her just like people judged me. I shook off my thoughts and gave her a genuine smile this time. "And you must be Cindy. It's very nice to meet you."

"Likewise." She nodded. "Now if you'll follow me, we'll get started."

I did as I was told, forming the questions I wanted to ask to confirm Gary's alibi. We entered a room even more tranquil than the lobby, with dim lights and essential oils pouring out of diffusers, and my footsteps slowed. "Wait, I'm sorry if I gave you the wrong idea. I'm not here for a massage. I'm here to interview you." I really didn't like to be touched. It was a different story with my Detective Grumpy Pants, but he was the only one I'd ever felt comfortable with.

She turned around and looked me over carefully. "Honey, you're not the only one who is good at reading people. I'm a massage therapist, and judging by the tension in your shoulders, you need my help more than you know." She handed me a sheet, told me to get undressed, lie down on the table, and cover up with the sheet.

I blinked. "No, I... I mean, I really don't have time for—"

"Nonsense. You of all people should know the importance of taking care of oneself. Let me help you, and I'll answer any questions you want to ask me. Deal?"

I'd never had a massage because I'd heard horror stories on how painful they were, but I was here to get answers. If that involved going through a bit of torture, then so be it. "Deal."

Ten minutes later, I lay face down on the massage table feeling exposed and vulnerable in my birthday suit. Granted all my girlie parts were covered by the sheet and my massage therapist was a woman, but still. I hated not knowing what to expect.

Cindy came in and her voice transformed into a hypnotic, comforting tone, and I felt myself relaxing. Some heavenly-smelling warm oil dripped onto my back, and then the most incredible thing happened. Magical hands pressed firmly onto my muscles, manipulating them skillfully until they released any tension they harbored and became pliant blobs of Jello. I groaned, feeling like I was under a spell.

"Congratulations, by the way. I heard you're engaged," Cindy said. I tensed up for a moment, but she quickly moved to my shoulders and got them to relax once more. "Touchy subject?"

I sighed. "No, not really. I mean, don't get me

wrong. I love Detective Stone more than anything." I found myself spilling everything, which was so unlike me to a complete stranger, but I couldn't seem to stop myself. Maybe because she *was* a stranger, and I really needed to talk to someone. "He wants me to set a date, but I want children, and he's not sure if he does. That means we're at an impasse. I can't set a date until we figure out if this is a deal-breaker or not. We've decided to table the topic until this murder case is solved."

"That's not a bad idea. I find a little distance from a conversation can bring the clarity you're looking for. At least you're smart to put your cards on the table before the wedding. I didn't do that with my ex-husband, and now we're divorced. He wanted children and wanted me to be a stay-at-home mom."

"Oh, so you didn't want children?"

"On the contrary. I love children, but I also love my career. I don't see why I can't have both. I was willing to compromise, but he wouldn't budge on his expectations. He couldn't accept me working at all, but he really couldn't handle that my career involved touching naked people, especially other men. It makes me so angry when people call me a masseuse and relate what I do to a sexual experience. I'm a massage therapist, skilled at healing the human body. I look at the human body the same way a doctor would. There's nothing sexual about it. That's why I moved to Divinity. To start fresh and work on changing that stereotype."

"I get it, believe me. I'm so tired of trying to get people to take what I do seriously. They think fortune-telling is all for show, but I use my fortune-telling tools to tap into my psychic ability. No matter how many times I've helped the police or proven my readings to be accurate, there are many who still don't take me seriously."

"Including Mitch?" Cindy asked softly.

"He's coming around. He can't deny some of the things I've seen, but he's still not a true believer. That's another thing I have to decide if I can live with or not."

"No wonder you were so tense." She patted my shoulder. "All set."

I rolled over, wrapping the sheet around me as I sat up to face her, realizing my body was pain free. I felt like cooked spaghetti, all limp and wobbly. "Holy cow, now I understand why Gary is so obsessed with you," I mumbled.

Her hands hesitated for a moment, and then she resumed washing them. "You really think he likes me?" She dried her hands and faced me, her cheeks as pink as her hair.

"I know so," I said with confidence. "He'll come around and say 'yes' to your offer of investing in his business. He has big dreams; he's just never had anyone believe in him until you."

"I think he's an amazing man. And his business has so much potential. It's a sound investment."

"I agree. I told him as much. You're good for him. And I'm beginning to think he's good for you."

Her eyes widened. "Are you getting a reading from me?"

"Nah, it's just written all over your face." I studied her. "You light up when his name is mentioned."

The pink deepened. "I won't deny that. So, what did you want to ask me?"

"The main thing I need to verify is, was Gary with you the day of the murder of Gunther Corp?"

"Yes," she answered without hesitation. "He was stressed out over the altercation with Gunther and

Cole in his back room, and came to me that morning for a massage, but I was all booked up. So, I told him to come back in a couple hours. He did, and told me all about it while I gave him a massage. People tend to open up to me when they're relaxed."

"I can attest to that," I chuckled.

"After that, we were talking much the same as you and I are now, and that's when I offered to invest in his business. I can tell you for sure, he was here until well after Gunther was murdered. He just hasn't given me an answer yet."

"I have a feeling you'll be hearing from him soon." I slid off the table, keeping my sheet tight around me. "Thank you so much for the therapy today. My body feels much lighter."

"I'm glad I could help. And thank you for the vote of confidence regarding Gary. I'll leave you to get dressed now. Oh, and make sure you drink plenty of fluids to release the toxins from your body."

"Will do." Cindy left and I got dressed, happy to clear Gary's name, but more worried than ever for Cole. My body might be relaxed, but my mind was more of a mess than ever. We were running out of options, and we still hadn't found the biggest toxin of all.

Gunther's Corp's killer.

A COUPLE DAYS LATER, I HEADED TO MY PARENTS' INN. I still couldn't wrap my brain around the fact that my parents were retired and had bought Divine Inspiration. Snowflakes softly fell, casting the inn under an enchanting glow. I couldn't get over the progress my mother had made on whipping the inn into shape in time for Winterfest. A spring opening had been ambi-

tious, but opening in February had been a nearly impossible feat. Just goes to show what money can do.

And my parents had plenty.

Work crews of all sorts covered the grounds from
counties across the state. There were men working on
the roof, others working on the siding, some on the
front porch, many working on the grounds and equipment shed. My gaze scanned the entire area, impressed. Then I did a double take.

"Dad? What on earth are you and Harry doing?"

"As head of the grounds crew, good ol' Harry and I
are doing our due diligence and testing out the new
equipment." He stood in a pair of cross-country skis,
see-sawing his legs back and forth across the snow, his
ski poles anchoring him in place.

"But you don't know how to ski." Good Lord, the
man didn't have an athletic bone in his body. "You're
going to pull something if you're not careful. And
since when did the inn have recreational equipment?"

"Since your mother and I took over. We need more
of a draw to get people to visit the inn. We wanted to
offer more than just ice fishing. Harry says it's good to
become one with nature."

I was beginning to see what my mother meant
about *Harry says*. "Well, Harry shouldn't be on a pair
of skis either. He's old enough to be your father."

"No worries, dear," Harry chimed in, startling me
from behind as he joined my father on a pair of snowshoes. "Age is just a number, and I'm fitter than men
half my age, but even I know my limits." He tapped his
snowshoe with his pole and winked at me.

Just then, the sound of an engine roared to life. I
whipped my head to the side to see Frank LaLone, the
inn's maintenance man, sitting on a snowmobile. He
pointed at the Wonder Twins and shrugged as he con-

tinued to test out their latest toy they claimed was also for the guests, but something told me it had more to do with checking off further items on their bucket lists.

My mother came running out the front door, her hand patting her chest in fright, then she scowled when she saw the snowmobile making all that racket. Her arms started flailing about and her lips were moving furiously, but you couldn't understand a word she said above the noise.

Everything happened at once.

Frank cut the engine, Dad's pole slipped, he started scissoring across the lawn, Mom screamed, and then Dad plowed her over on his out-of-control ride to the edge of the yard before disappearing into the trees. Harry trotted off after him, high stepping all the way, trying to get the hang of his snowshoes while hollering apologies to my mother.

Good Lord, what next?

I ran over to my mother and helped her up. "Are you okay?"

"Yes, darling, but your father won't be once I get ahold of him. He's lucky I have the bones of a woman half my age. Have you seen his latest endeavor? Winter amenities. Every time I make some headway on the inn, he sets us back with his cockamamie ideas. He doesn't have a clue what he's doing. The man is going to get himself killed or kill someone else."

"Oh goodness, don't say that. One parent accused of murder is all I can handle in this lifetime."

"Don't be silly." She brushed the snow off her impeccable clothes. "I was never in any danger of going to jail. We all knew I was innocent."

She had been closer to jail than she realized, and *we* all didn't know anything. She had despised the innkeeper. She was just lucky that someone despised her more, and got sloppy. If we hadn't caught the cake lady, my mother most likely would be spending the rest of her life behind bars. I didn't need to worry about my father now, too.

The sound of Mitch's truck pulling into the driveway brought a smile to my face. No matter our issues, I was always happy to see him.

"Ah, now there's a sensible man." My mother tipped her head to Mitch as he approached us.

"Vivian." He leaned forward and kissed her cheek, then pulled me in for a hug. His gaze scanned the yard and he raised a jet-black brow as he looked at me.

I shook my head slightly and mouthed, *don't ask.*

"Let's go inside. It's freezing out here." My mother led the way through the front door.

Mitch whispered, "Where's your father?"

"You don't want to know," I responded.

The inside of the inn was just as busy, with all sorts of people making the final touches on the walls, ceilings, and floors. The place looked amazing. Only my mother would have the resources and reinforcements to complete the job in record time. Winterfest started in a couple days, and by then she would be fully prepared to open her doors.

"I have to admit, you did it, Mom. The place looks incredible."

Granny and Fiona bustled around the room, offering cookies and drinks to the workers, totally in their element. And it didn't look like any of the workers minded, based on their grateful smiles. Just then Great-Grandma Tootsie walked out of the kitchen with a huge tray of finger sandwiches, as a bearded giant held the door for her.

"What the hell is he doing here," Mitch grumbled,

clenching his teeth as he made a beeline for the newcomer.

I hurried beside him.

"Why, Detective Stone, it's so good to see you again. Though your face looks a little sour. Here, have a sandwich."

"Sorry, Grandma Tootsie, I've lost my appetite."

"Well, that's too bad. Take a couple antacids. They'll fix you up right as rain. Hey, did you meet my new friend?"

"Oh, we've met." Mitch glared at Ralph Peters, better known as Tow Truck Guy, aka the man who left us stranded in a ditch.

"Bless my stars. Isn't he a peach?"

"He's something, all right." I took Mitch's hand and gave it a squeeze.

"I met him in Gretta's Mini Mart when I couldn't reach the top shelf, darn this old, crooked back of mine. He was so kind. He followed me through the whole store, helping me reach all the items on my list, bless his soul. Well, I best be on my way. Those poor youngins must be half starved to death by now."

"That's a good idea, Toots. We'll just borrow your friend here for a moment," I said.

"Oh, I'm sure he won't mind one bit. He's so helpful." She went on her way, humming The Lawrence Welk show theme song with every step.

"You heard, Toots. Maybe it's time you start being *helpful*, Ralph. And you can begin by telling me what you're doing in Divinity?"

"I don't have to tell you anything." Ralph straightened to his full, frightening height.

I stepped between my steaming detective and the smirking giant. "Actually, Mr. Peters, you kind of do, since this is a murder investigation, and you're a suspect."

His bushy eyebrows drew together in a deep V, his smirk all but gone as he rubbed the top of his bald head. "How do you figure?"

"Well, your wife was having an affair with the victim. You found out and retaliated by killing him. And now you're back to kill your wife."

The first flash of genuine pain crossed the giant's features. "I would never harm Kristen. I always knew she was too good for me, but I never thought she'd actually cheat." His jaw hardened. "And now I think she's cheating again with Ray Simone. I followed them here, but that's all. When Grandma Tootsie needed help, I couldn't say no." His face softened. "She reminds me of my own grandmother, God rest her soul."

"I don't suppose you know anything about the recent break-ins of some local stores?" Mitch stared him down.

"Despite how I look, I'm a lover, not a fighter, Detective."

"And not a very good tow truck driver." Mitch huffed. "You left us stranded."

"I don't know what you're talking about." Ralph inspected his nails.

"Likely story," Mitch growled. "Stay put until I check out your story, and stay away from your wife and Simone or you'll find yourself stranded in my jail cell. Are we clear?"

"As the ice in your heart."

"Good." Mitch headed for the front door.

"Detective?" Ralph said almost reluctantly.

"Yeah?" Mitch turned back to Ralph.

"The only place I haven't searched is the campgrounds," he admitted. "Is that helpful enough for you?"

Mitch nodded once, then turned around and opened the door.

"Where are you going?" I asked, hot on his heels.

"To see a man about a tent."

12

"Captain's not gonna like this, Tink. We're supposed to be dividing and conquering. You could have stayed at the inn to keep an eye on Ralph." Mitch pulled into the parking lot of the campgrounds just outside of Mini Central Park.

"I have a feeling he's all bark and no bite. He's just an upset husband. Besides, Great-Grandma Tootsie will keep him plenty busy. He won't have time to get into trouble." I reached over and held Mitch's hand. "Besides, we've barely seen each other lately. I miss you."

He lifted my hand to his mouth and kissed the backs of my fingers. "Me too, babe." His gaze met mine and held. "We'll talk soon. I promise."

"I know." I leaned over and kissed him. "Let's go see that man about a tent." We climbed out of his truck and headed to the campground office. "Although, who tents in the middle of winter?"

"I didn't mean an actual tent. It was just a figure of speech. The campgrounds are closed during winter, but I wouldn't put it past Ray to sneak into a cabin."

"Okay, then." I rubbed my palms together. "You

take the east end and I'll take the west, then we'll meet in the middle."

The detective was already shaking his head. "Hell, no. We're not splitting up, Tink."

"Divide and conquer, remember?" I poked him in the chest.

He caught my hand. "Not happening."

"Listen, Mitch, I'll be fine." I huffed out a breath, the steam streaming in a smokey cloud between us. "It's broad daylight, and you won't be far. If we don't split up, we'll never get through searching all the cabins before dark. We both have our phones, and you're my number one speed dial."

"I'd better be," he grumbled.

"I'll call you if I get into trouble."

He grunted. "When *don't* you get into trouble?"

"Funny." I smirked. "Besides, Morty always shows up when I need help. You know that. In fact, I sense his presence right now." I didn't, but I knew that was the only way Grumpy Pants would let me help.

He hesitated, not looking happy in the least, but then he blew out a heavy breath and pointed his finger at me. "Keep that phone in your hand at all times."

"Done." I tightened my coat and headed west, not daring to look back for fear Mitch would change his mind.

An hour later, after searching cabin after cabin with no luck, I began to lose hope of finding anything. I couldn't get discouraged or give up. Cole needed us to find a clue that might take the suspicion off of him before the mayor made us close the case. So I kept trudging through the snow, one boot in front of the other.

The snow crunched beneath my feet, the wind

whistling through the trees overhead. The swan pond was in the middle of the park. There wasn't anything out here except woods. The type of people who rented these remote cabins preferred isolation...

Or had something to hide.

I had to be nearing the center, but I didn't hear Mitch coming. I stopped before yet another cabin and tried the door. It was unlocked. I peeked through the dirty window but didn't see any movement, so I walked inside carefully, and Bingo! Clothes were strewn around the room, the bed was unmade, and the wood stove was still warm. I was guessing the belongings were Ray and Kristen's. It looked as though whoever had stayed here left in a hurry. Maybe someone had tipped them off that Mitch and I were snooping around.

Taking another step toward a chair, I picked up a woman's sweater. My body jerked and my vision narrowed into tunnel vision like it always did when I had a vision. I felt myself fade into a trancelike state. A man and a woman stood in this very room, but I couldn't see their faces clearly. My breathing picked up and I felt like I was on the verge of hyperventilating. Paralyzing fear gripped me.

"He's going to find out. I just know he is," a female voice said.

"Stop stressing, woman," the male voice growled. "You're giving me a headache."

"I can't help it. We're in danger if he finds out. You know that, right?"

"You let me worry about him. But you need to stop acting suspicious."

"Easier said than done. What if he finds us?"

"I'm through with this cat-and-mouse crap. Maybe it's time we find him."

"Wait, now?"

"Yes, now. And I think I know where to look. It's—"

"Sunny. Sunny, wake up!" Hands gripped my shoulders and shook.

I blinked several times until my eyes adjusted. Mitch stood before me, looking worried. Well, shoot. I had been so close. Just one more minute. I sighed and my shoulders slumped, releasing the tension from bunching them up.

"I don't think I'll ever get used to seeing you come out of one of your visions." He shuddered. "Scares the hell out of me every time."

"Why?" I asked absently, picking up another article of clothing. Nothing. Not even a flicker of a reading.

"I'm afraid one of these days you're not going to return to me." His tone filled with genuine worry.

My eyes met his. I wanted to say "I'll always return to you," but what if it wasn't true? What if we couldn't get past this issue between us? "It's okay. I know what I'm doing," I finally responded.

He narrowed his eyes. "If you're okay, then why did Morty show up?"

I scanned the cabin with a smile. "He did?"

Mitch scrubbed a hand over his head. "I couldn't find you anywhere and I kept calling your name, but you didn't answer. Don't you ever scare me like that again, by the way." A muscle in his jaw bulged, straining the scar beneath his whiskers.

"I will do my best not to, but I can't make any promises." I lifted my hands, palms up. "Where's Morty now?"

"When you didn't answer, he appeared by my side and led the way to the cabin. I found you standing there in a trance, then Morty left."

"Aha. That should tell you right there." I patted Mitch's chest. "He knew I was fine. If he thought I was in any *real* danger, he would have stayed."

"Or maybe," my detective patted the top of my head, "he's—"

"Hey, stop that. I'm not a dog."

"—beginning to trust that I love you as much as he does." He tweaked my nose.

Everything in me softened. "I really am okay, Mitch. I know I feel everything the person goes through when I have a vision, but I've come to accept that's empathy. These things didn't actually happen to me. It's how I cope."

"Tell me everything," he said as we headed back to his truck.

"There was a man and a woman who stayed in that cabin recently. I couldn't see the faces of either clearly. I can't tell if it's Ray and Kristen or not. If it is, then it looks like Ralph might be right. They might be having an affair."

"It sure seems that way." Mitch kicked ice balls of snow out of the way and lifted tree branches aside as we walked.

"Well, I felt real fear from the woman, but not toward the man. She kept referring to another man she was afraid would find out what they were doing. That makes me think they were talking about Ralph." I chewed the inside of my cheek for a minute as I thought about it. "Yet the man with her kept getting annoyed at her, which didn't seem like a man who was smitten."

"Maybe it's not about love." Mitch spoke with a funny tone, and I glanced at him. His cheeks flushed ever so slightly. "They could still be having an affair.

Maybe, uh, maybe they're simply meeting each other's needs." He shrugged but didn't make eye contact.

"Maybe." I bit back a chuckle, then sobered as I contemplated the vision. "She said the other man was looking for them, which Ralph is, but could someone else be looking for them, too? And if they're not talking about an affair or Ralph, then who are they talking about and what don't they want him to discover?"

"Only one way to find out." He opened the truck door for me as I nodded in agreement.

"Find Ralph and Kristen A.S.A.P."

MITCH AND I PARKED ALONG MAIN STREET AT THE END, so we could walk the entire street and talk to the vendors. They were our best bet for finding out if Ray and Kristen were in town. The streets were already full of outsiders and it was only day one of Winterfest. The parade that kicked off the festival had finished hours ago, and the sun was already sinking. Upstate NY in the wintertime got dark around five p.m., so we didn't have much time left.

"Ah, I see Detective Fuller down by Smokey Jo's. I'm going to catch up with him to see if he has any leads on Officer Adam Burrows, and I'll meet you inside when you're done." Mitch kissed my cheek then took off down the street at a jog.

I stopped and talked to Pricilla at Pricilla's Paintings stand to show a picture of Kristen Peters and Ray Simone, but she hadn't seen them around. Pricilla was a regular every year with the most spectacular paintings of nature. The next booth belonged to a man named

Quincy. He was also a regular who came every year to display his unique pieces of blown glass in his Glassworks stand. When I questioned him, he hadn't seen them or the Rebel Riders. Either Ray and Kristen were doing a good job of laying low, or they really weren't in town. But if they weren't in town, then who was doing all the break-ins? And if nothing was being stolen, then what was the point, other than to send a message: Pay up for protection or things might get ugly?

Crossing the street, I saw Eileen Bucktown at her Lake & Pebble Art stand. Her stand was situated on the curb in front of Warm Beginnings and Cozy Endings. She stood outside talking to Natalie Kirsch, the café owner. I waited for a pause in their conversation before interrupting.

"Hi, ladies. How's the first day of Winterfest treating you?" I studied a pair of pebble earrings, impressed with the quality of the craftsmanship.

"Surprisingly well, all things considered," Eileen responded. "I was a little worried sales would be down because of the festival attendance being down due to the ongoing murder investigation, but I've had a steady flow of customers all day."

"That's great. Mayor Cromwell isn't happy that Detective Stone hasn't wrapped up the case yet. This festival brings in a lot of money, and he doesn't want anything interfering with that."

"Anyone who knows Cole West very well at all would know he's not a murderer," Natalie chimed in. "Poor Jo must be a total mess, what with her babies due any time now and the possibility of their daddy going to jail."

"Mitch won't let that happen," I said as much to reassure myself as I did them. "That's why he's being so thorough. He won't close this case until he discovers the truth. Speaking of trauma, how are you holding up after the break-in to your café?" I glanced beyond her and noticed the window had been repaired.

"I'm doing okay. I'm more frustrated than anything. The vandals didn't steal a thing. They just cost me a lot of money in damages. Everybody thinks it's the Rebel Riders, after what they did to Gary's Hardware Store. But Smokey Jo's and Sam's Bakery and my café were hit after Gunther Corp's murder. The Rebel Riders haven't been seen since that day."

"I've been thinking the same thing. If it wasn't them, then who was it? And why? Did the crime scene investigators discover anything?"

"Just a few strands of blond hair. They sent the hair off to be tested for DNA. Hopefully we'll have some answers soon."

I patted her shoulder. "I hope so. And, hey, can you let me know if anything else turns up?"

"Sure thing."

"Oh, and have either of you seen these two around town in the past few days?" I showed Ray and Kristen's pictures.

Natalie shook her head no, but Eileen's eyebrows crept up. "Actually, a woman who looked a lot like that picture stopped into my booth just a little while ago and bought a pair of earrings. She paid cash. The man wasn't with her."

"Thank you." I handed them both my card. "Please call me immediately if you see either of them again." Well, at least I'd confirmed that Kristen was most definitely in Divinity, but what was she doing alone? Where was Ray?

They both nodded in agreement as they took my card, and I headed over to Smokey Jo's. The sun had almost completely set now and most festival attendees had gone home. The air had a bite to it that had me tightening my coat with every step. My footsteps faltered, and I searched the area, having a tingling feeling that I was being watched. I didn't see anything out of the ordinary, but my gut was never wrong when it came to my heightened senses. I picked up the pace.

Mitch stood outside of Smokey Jo's in front of Wayne's Woodworks booth, talking to Detective Fuller and Wayne Emerson. Wayne held a rag under his bloody nose, and several pieces of wooden items were broken and scattered on the ground. I studied the items closely, being a big lover of crafts. They weren't very good, but who was I to judge? I didn't have a crafty bone in my body.

"Are you sure you didn't recognize the man who did this to you?" Fuller questioned Wayne as he flipped through the details in his notebook.

"No, I told you I've never seen him before. Then again, I'm new to Winterfest, so it could be someone local for all I know. He wanted a piece of my art. We haggled over the price, and when I wouldn't budge any lower, he smashed several pieces. I tried to stop him and he punched me in the face, then left in a hurry. That's when Mrs. West called you," Wayne said to Fuller.

Mitch frowned, probably wondering the same thing I did. Why didn't Jo call Mitch? I was hoping she wasn't losing faith in him as a detective and just didn't want to distract him from the murder investigation that would hopefully clear her husband's name.

"Since I'm late to the party, I missed all the details," Mitch said. "Did you get a description of the man?"

"He was alone at first. Short, stocky, tough-looking.

Then after the incident, a woman showed up beside him wearing a leather jacket with an RR on it, and they took off."

Mitch's gaze cut to mine, then back to Wayne's. He pulled out a picture and showed it to him. "Do you recognize these people?"

Wayne's eyes widened. "That's them. Who are they?"

"Ray Simone and Kristen Peters, wanted suspects in the death of Gunther Corp."

"Oh, boy," I said, drawing Mitch's gaze. "Mayor Cromwell isn't going to be happy about this."

"About what?" Wayne asked, looking worried.

I shook my head. "Looks like the Rebel Riders haven't left town after all."

13

"That's amazing, Jo," I said after sampling her chili recipe for the cookoff at the end of the festival. A mix of sweet and spicey flavors burst over my tongue, with a hint of smokey sausage thrown in with the beef.

"I concur," Mitch responded around a mouthful, and kept shoveling in more spoonfuls between moans of pleasure.

Jo slid a longneck bottle of beer down the bar, stopping exactly in front of me. Then she set three fingers of whiskey in front of Mitch.

He raised his glass in salute, then took a hefty sip and sighed. He closed his eyes for a moment, listening to the soothing sounds of Seventies folk music filling the room. It had been a long day without much progress. "I hope you know I'm not giving up on the case."

Jo frowned, rubbing her enormous belly. "Of course we know. Why would you ask?"

He paused from eating long enough to look her in the eye. "You called Detective Fuller instead of me when the fight happened out front."

"Of course, she did," Cole chimed in, as he restocked the glasses behind the bar. "I'm pretty sure the murder investigation is a full-time job. The last thing we want to do is distract you at all."

"That's what we figured," I said. "We just wanted to make sure you both knew we're doing everything we can to solve this case, and we won't stop until we do."

"Crazy what happened to Wayne Emerson," Miles said as he moved from his table to the bar and took a seat next to Mitch. Zoe bused his table, taking the dishes in the back to Sean. Cole handed Miles a beer, and he saluted in thanks. "I remember the Rebel Riders, and when you went back to them. I always thought Gunther Corp had a screw loose. I don't blame anyone for killing him. The man was downright dangerous." Miles shook his blond head, looking so much like his sister Faith it was uncanny.

"We all know you're innocent, Cole." Zack joined Miles a couple seats down with Morty on his lap. He'd relaxed considerably since Morty had become his service animal, which still amazed me. "Justice will prevail. You'll see." Cole handed him tequila, and Zack downed the shot on a wince. Morty jumped and then meowed at me. "Sorry, buddy. I didn't mean to scare you," Zack said, and stroked his sleek white back.

Since when did Morty scare?

"I sure hope so." Miles tipped his beer up for a long swig. "It would be a damn shame if justice doesn't prevail. And damned unfair."

"From your lips to the judge's ears." Cole took a rare shot of his own, then rubbed the chain link tattoo surrounding his thick neck. "I can't go to prison. I just can't."

"Enough with the dreary attitude. None of us can afford to give up hope." Cole's secretary Cathy held her head high and nodded once at Cole as she sat beside Zack. "I have complete faith that Detective Stone and Ms. Meadows will figure this whole mess out. Have you found the murder weapon yet?" she asked Mitch.

"Not yet, but there's only so many places to hide something like that in Divinity. It will turn up, I'm sure."

"I still can't figure out how it got out of my safe." Cole scrubbed his buzzed head, lifting his broad shoulders.

"Are you positive you didn't take it out and misplace it, then forget about it?" I asked, hoping he would remember something. Anything.

"It's my *gun*, Sunny. I would no more lose track of that than Mitch would his."

"You've got a point." The scar along Mitch's jaw pulsed as he stared off in thought for a moment. "It had to be someone who knew how to handle a weapon."

"And someone who knew Cole," Jo added.

"Actually, everyone in town knows Cole has a concealed-carry license since his correctional officer days, so it's likely to assume he has a gun safe."

"But who would know the combination?" I asked.

"Most locks can be picked, Tink. Once we figure out who might have the know-how, then we just might have a case."

———

THE NEXT DAY JO, ZOE, AND I WATCHED THE ICE sculpting contest after lunch. I'd had a couple clients first thing in the morning, but my afternoon was free. Winterfest drew locals and outsiders alike, and no one wanted to miss the ice sculpting contest. Amazing creations were formed, ranging from a train, a mama bear with cubs, the Statue of Liberty, and many other detailed objects. Sam the baker was the winner with his perfect replica of our resident swans, Fred and Ginger, on Inspiration Lake in Mini Central Park.

Kids were making snow angels and having snow-ball fights along the sides of Main Street, while the cross-country ski race was setting up in the road. There was enough snowpack, and the road had been blocked off since this morning. The entrants took their position at the starting line, most of them with ski rentals from the inn. Harry stood at the ready to send them off, while my father stood at the finish line at the edge of the ribbon tied across the street, ready to call the winner. At least they hadn't been foolish enough to enter themselves after their crazy trip through the woods.

My mother still hadn't forgiven my father for knocking her over.

Harry held his hand up high in the air with the blank gun pointing to the sky. "On your mark," he called.

Everyone shifted their stance.

"Get ready," he added in dramatic fashion.

People dug in their poles.

"Go!" He fired the gun, and the racers took off.

Everyone pushed off the starting line, scissoring their legs forward and backward, trying to get ahead of their competitors at any cost. There were nudges of shoulders and bumps of hips and poles slipping into skis. People were crazy when it came to a com-petition. The collective energy from the festival and the spectators watching the race was positive and happy. Everyone's mood seemed to match the beauty of the day, and as I glanced to Jo, my hope was renewed that we would find our killer and clear Cole's name. As the skiers neared the finish line, my father stood holding the finish-line pole as he stared straight across to be sure he could see exactly who won.

The ribbon broke and my father threw his hands in the air, shouting the number of the winner. Turns out it was Wally of Wally's World gym. No surprise there. My father shook his hand and handed him a trophy. That was when I saw her.

Kristen Peters.

I'd never met her, but I'd seen enough pictures to know it was definitely her. I scanned the area but didn't see Ray Simone.

"I'll catch up with you girls later," I said, keeping my eyes on Kristen. "There's something I have to do."

Jo and Zoe waved me off, then headed over to join my mother and Fiona. Granny Gert and Great-Grandma Tootsie had stayed behind with Ralph Peters to hold down the fort at the inn.

I hurried my steps and caught up to Kristen just as she left the Knitting Nanas' booth and entered the booth run by the Sewing Sisters. She was eyeing a quilt as I walked up to her. She smiled at me then kept browsing.

"Beautiful work, isn't it?" I asked, inspecting a blanket with cats stitched across it that I had my eye on.

"All the booths are very impressive this year." She glanced towards Wayne's Woodworks and frowned. "Well, most of the booths anyway."

I followed her gaze. "Ah, yes. I heard the man was new to the festival, but I haven't bought any of his material yet."

"Don't waste your time. It's not very good."

So I wasn't the only one who thought his work wasn't very good.

"And the man is rude. He made a crude pass at me."

Interesting. Wayne hadn't mentioned that part. "Really? That must have been uncomfortable."

"It sure was."

"What did you do?"

"When I rebuked his advances, he got really angry with me and then started arguing with my friend."

I picked up another blanket, inspecting the stitch work. "I heard a man punched Mr. Emerson in the face. Gave him a bloody nose and smashed his goods."

"He deserved the bloody nose after how he was acting. And *he* is the one who smashed the goods, not my friend. The man flew into such a rage out of nowhere. It was scary. The man's unstable if you ask me. We got out of there before he could do anything else."

"I'm Sunny Meadows, by the way." I held out my arm.

"Kristen." She shook my hand.

"Kristen...?"

She hesitated a moment, studying me closer then dropped my hand. "Just Kristen."

I smiled. "Where's your friend? Maybe I've met him."

"Who knows? He's around here somewhere." She inspected a set of placemats. "The man can't sit still and hates to shop. I'm sure I'll find him later."

"You don't mind if your husband leaves you alone in a strange town?" I stared down at the rings on her left-hand ring finger.

"Oh, no, he's not my husband." She shoved her hands in her coat pockets.

"Ah, I see." I picked up a shawl, admiring the pattern.

"We're just friends," she hastened to add. "Well, I better get moving. I think the snowmobile race is going to start in thirty minutes, and I want a front row seat." She started walking away in a hurry.

"It was nice to meet you." I caught up with her. "If you ever need to talk, my house is right on the outskirts of town." I handed her my card.

She studied my business card. "You're a psychic?"

I nodded.

"I really do need to go, but I might take you up on that sometime."

"My door is always open." I smiled and waved, then headed to rent some equipment from my father. Forget about a front row seat. I had a race to enter.

THIS TIME MY FATHER STOOD AT THE STARTING LINE, and Harry was positioned at the finish line. Didn't matter how old a man got, they were still boys on the inside who loved playing with their toys. I looked down the row of entrants, but it was impossible to tell who they were. They all wore dark helmets with tinted glass and bulky snowsuits. Good thing I had asked the inn's maintenance man, Frank LaLone, to show me how all the equipment worked in case my father needed help. Still, I'd never actually driven one of these.

How hard could it be?

My father held the gun high in the air and counted us down, then pulled the trigger with a huge smile on his face. My mother flinched at the sound and plugged her ears. I would have laughed if I wasn't terrified. Grumpy Pants was going to be livid once he found out what I'd done, but there was no turning back now. We'd been looking for Ray with no success. There was only one reason Kristen Peters was so excited to go to the snowmobile races. She must have known he would enter.

Everyone hit the throttle and took off into the woods. There were trails that went around the lake and ended up back in town at the finish line. I stalled my machine, but quickly got it started again. That put me in last place. Once I got the hang of things, I gunned the engine. It wasn't long before I caught up to the others. The trail was barely wide enough to pass. I noticed many people doing so, and moving up their place to the finish line. I did the same until I realized one entrant dressed all in black never even tried to pass. In fact, if I wasn't mistaken, he looked to be slowing down.

Maybe he had engine trouble? I thought about stopping, but something gave me pause. So, I kept moving forward and blew past him. He fell way behind until he disappeared out of sight. I rounded the next corner, once again behind the others because I'd been paying attention to the man in black. Suddenly, Morty was in front of me on a side trail, just sitting there, staring at me. I immediately stopped, but then he raced down the side trail. I tried to catch up to him, but he had vanished.

Crazy cat would get himself home. I'd stopped worrying about him after the first week he'd adopted me. We all knew Vicky, the ancient Victorian house I'd bought, was his and he'd decided to let me stay. We were kindred spirits. If he were in real trouble, I would know. The only reason I could think of for why he had appeared is that he was trying to tell me something.

I heard the sound of a snowmobile up ahead, so I slowed down and stopped behind a patch of trees. Bingo. Morty had shown me the way. The man in black came in from a side trail and headed even deeper into the woods away from the race. I followed at a safe distance. Looking further ahead, I sucked in a breath. He was headed to the cabin I had searched. When he pulled up beside it, I turned into the woods and cut my engine at the same time so he wouldn't hear me. He took off his helmet and scanned the area. I knew it!

Ray Simone.

I could tell even from this far away that it was Ray. He was built like a Mac truck. There was no mistaking his stature. It had been ingrained on my brain from the moment I'd met him and Gunther outside of Nikko's restaurant that fateful day. I stayed hidden amongst the trees as I traipsed through the woods to get a closer look.

He went inside the cabin, so I picked up the pace. Maybe Kristen had lied and really left the festival to go back to the cabin and meet him. But I could have sworn I saw her in the front row like she said she'd be. I kept moving forward, picking up a stick to use as a weapon if need be. I stopped at the edge of the woods by a snow-covered road.

That's when I heard the car.

Ducking back under the cover of the trees, I waited. A woman exited the car and walked to the cabin door. She wore a different coat than Kristen, but it was hard to tell if it was her from this distance. Maybe she'd changed once she got in the car. Ray opened the door, his face sporting a cocky grin, and he kissed the woman smack on the lips. He stepped back and had her take off her coat and twirl before him.

The woman was most definitely *not* Kristen Peters.

She was dressed in a sexy, tight, slinky silver number with deep auburn waves of hair. Ray definitely had a type. She looked similar to Kristen, but younger. Besides, Kristen said she and Ray were just friends. This woman looked *extra* friendly based on her body language. He brought her inside and closed the door. That was my cue to leave.

We were in the middle of a race, after all. People were bound to notice if the man in black and the woman in red, aka me, didn't return. They—meaning Detective Grumpy Pants—would come looking for sure. So, I quickly made my way back to my snowmobile and started her up.

The cabin door flew open and Ray came running out, searching the area. His hard stare landed on me.

Well, shoot.

I hit the throttle, praying I wouldn't stall it this time, and bolted forward. It only took Ray a minute to throw his gear back on and follow me. He was a much better rider than I was. It didn't take him long to catch up to me. He tried to pass me, but I veered left. Then he tried for the right and almost made it, but my sled sideswiped him and I remained in front.

Sorry, Dad.

One last push. He was almost on top of me. I could tell he intended to ram into me before we cleared the woods and came back into town. I gave the engine everything I had and exploded out of the woods just in time, my skis skidding in a full circle until I got the sled back under control and crossed the finish line seconds before Ray.

I came to a stop, my hands shaking as I took off my helmet. A beat of awkward silence hung in the chilly air before the crowd went wild. My father was over the moon, while my mother was oddly speechless with her jaw hanging open in a most unladylike fashion. I obviously didn't win, but I didn't come in last, either, which was hardly the point. I hadn't entered this race caring about what position I finished in. I simply wanted answers, but I would let my family have their moment. Fiona twirled about, hopping up and down in glee. Granny Gert would be upset about missing the show, as I was sure Fiona would relish in reliving the details.

Ray peeled off his helmet and met my gaze with a steely one of his own. *Oh, boy.* Back to reality. Now he knew I was at the cabin and had seen him with his *other* woman. Kristen ran over to his side with a questioning expression on her face until she followed his gaze to me. Her eyes widened like a deer in the headlights. Then Mitch walked in my direction with purposeful strides and an angry look on his face.

Something told me I wasn't out of the woods just yet.

14

"Where were you the day Gunther Corp was murdered?" Detective Stone—he was most definitely not Mitch my fiancé today—sat behind the massive cherry desk in his office my mother had given him when they moved to Divinity. That desk had been with her throughout her law career, and she couldn't part with it. The inn didn't have a proper place for it—my mother's words—so she'd decided to keep it in the family by handing the stately piece of furniture over to her future son-in-law. I think it was her way of saying you deserve this for putting up with my daughter.

Ray Simone grunted from where he sat in the chair across from him.

A single picture of the two of us sat on his desk, and that was all. The rest of his office was stark and bare. He didn't believe in revealing much about himself, especially at work. That was something we were still working on.

Mitch hadn't talked to me about the snowmobile race or why we were so late. He'd immediately questioned Kristen, and she'd pretty much told him the same thing she had told me. She was friends with Ray, and that was all. He was helping her in her time of need because she was afraid of her husband, Ralph. She admitted she'd had an affair with Gunther because her husband was always working and helping others, neglecting her. Someone had anonymously tipped him off about the affair, and she'd never seen him so angry. She'd been hiding out with Ray in Divinity ever since. She just hadn't expected Ralph to follow.

Mitch told her not to leave town until the case was closed, but to stay away from Ralph. He didn't want any more altercations to happen, especially while Winterfest was going on. Now we were sitting in his office, questioning Ray. Rather, Detective Grumpy Pants was questioning Ray. I was only tagging along because Mitch didn't want me out of his sight, since apparently I couldn't be trusted not to put myself in danger.

"Look, Gunther and I didn't always see eye-to-eye," Ray responded. "We'd had a disagreement with the way the Rebel Riders should be run."

Mitch arched a shaggy eyebrow. "Yeah, like which business you were going to strong-arm next."

"That was Gunther's deal, not mine. I wanted to be legit, but Gunther was adamant he wanted to keep pressuring the businesses in Stillwater to pay for our protection."

"With Officer Burrows looking the other way, I'm sure it was a pretty sweet setup, even with the cut you had to pay him."

Ray's hands stilled in his lap. "You knew about that?"

Mitch leaned forward. "I know about a lot of things, Simone. So, don't even think about lying to me."

Hazard in the Horoscope

"Hey, I'm being straight with you. I thought, when Officer Burrows put an end to our business because of the Internal Affairs investigation, the situation would end. But no, Gunther insisted on moving on to a new town and starting over."

"Why Divinity?" Mitch flipped through his notes, then met Ray's eyes. "We're not a very big town. Your earning potential would be way less than in Stillwater, and I can tell you for a fact you won't have an inside man in the police department. I'm surprised Gunther didn't choose a neighboring town more the size of Stillwater."

"Someone tipped us off that Cole West was living in Divinity. That was all Gunther needed to hear." Ray rubbed the back of his neck, cracking it before he continued. "He was becoming unstable at the end. He was obsessed with getting revenge on Cole, and none of us could stop him. When Cole showed up at the Motorcycle Expo, I was out. I didn't want anything to do with the situation, so I left. When I heard Gunther was murdered, I checked out of the hotel, but I didn't leave town."

Detective Stone made a note in his book. "Is that when Kristen Peters approached you for help?"

Ray nodded. "We found the cabin and, well, you know the rest."

"We don't know the rest," I chimed in, earning a scowl from Grumpy Pants.

Ray focused on me for the first time, his eyes widening, then narrowing. His whole body tensed, and I could feel the anger flowing in waves off of him. If Mitch weren't here, I had no doubt Ray would hurt me.

"That's right," I said, shaking off my nerves. "I saw

you at the cabin with a woman, and she *wasn't* Kristen Peters."

"So?" He scowled. "I date a lot of women. It's not anyone's business but my own. Who cares anyway? *I'm* not the one who's married."

"I thought you said you were just friends," Mitch chimed in.

"Friends with benefits. Whatever you want to call it." Ray swiped his hand through the air. "I never claimed to be monogamous."

Ewww. "In the same cabin?" I cringed, earning a reproachful look from the Grumpster. We weren't here to judge. We were here to investigate. I knew that, but it was hard. I didn't like Ray, and my gut told me he was hiding something.

"Look, lady." His gaze ran over my disheveled appearance after coming straight from the snowmobile race. "I don't judge you. And last I checked, what I've done isn't a crime. Are we done here?" Ray began to rise from the chair.

"Sit down, we're not done." Mitch never looked up from his notes, adding, "We're just getting started." Ray dropped back into the chair, and Mitch leveled him with a hard look that would intimidate most. "Last I checked assaulting someone and destroying their property *is* a crime."

"Hey, I didn't destroy anything, man." Ray waved his hands before him. "I was minding my own business, checking out the dude's woodwork, when he starts hitting on Kristen. I get it. She's a beautiful woman. But the dude started taking things too far. I could tell she was uncomfortable, so I told him to knock it off. The man lost it. It was like someone had flipped a switch. The dude started smashing his woodwork, acting like a crazy man. Then he came at me, so I defended myself."

"By punching him in the face and breaking his nose? There's not a mark on you," I added. "Mr. Emerson might not be as tough as you, but he certainly looks like he could fight back at least a little."

"Look, I can't help it the dude didn't even try to fight back. One minute he's a crazy man, and the next he's a wimp. Maybe he has mental health issues or maybe he's on drugs? I don't know. It's the guy's word against mine, with no cameras or witnesses to prove otherwise. You don't have to worry about me. I don't plan on ever going back to his booth again."

"See that you don't," Mitch said.

"*Now* are we done?"

"Yeah, we're done," Mitch responded. "You'd better hope you're telling the truth about your gang not being behind the break-ins. You and your girlfriends stay put for now. I'll be in touch if I need to speak with any of you further."

Ray saluted him as he stood, then he gave me a parting glare that said, *You may have won the race, but this event isn't over by a long shot, sweetheart.*

THE NEXT MORNING, I WAS AT WARM BEGINNINGS AND Cozy Endings sipping a cup of tea. We were out of tea at home, and yes, I was avoiding a certain grumpy detective fiancé. He was heading into the office to meet with Captain Walker anyway. Something about a new lead. I had a free morning with no clients, but he didn't ask me to go with him. In fact, he was barely talking to me at all.

Natalie Kirsch came out of her office in the back

and spotted me. She joined me at my table and sat down, nursing a mug of coffee. "Hi, Sunny. How are you? I saw you in the snowmobile race. That was some wild ride."

"Oh, it was something, all right."

"I didn't know you were into sports, or whatever you call a race like that."

I laughed. "Neither did I."

She shook her head on a chuckle. "It sure made for an interesting event."

If she only knew the half of it. "Have you heard anything more on the hair sample they found after your break-in?"

"That's funny you should ask. I was actually meaning to call you. The report came back with an interesting bit of information."

"Really?" I leaned in.

Natalie looked left, then right around her café before she set her mug on the table, leaning forward as well. "The hair sample was no ordinary hair. It came from a wig. Can you believe it?" She picked her mug back up and blew on it before taking a sip.

"Thank you, Natalie." I finished my tea. "You just made my day."

She scrunched up her face. "How so?"

"Now I have something to do." I laid money on the table for my tea, then grabbed my fringed cross-body bag and headed for the door.

"Where are you going?"

"I'd say I'm overdue for a haircut."

PUMP UP THE VOLUME HAIR SALON WAS PACKED. I MADE my way to the reception desk. "Any chance I can speak to Raoulle?"

"Not unless you have an appointment." The young girl looked to be high school age, wearing her blond ponytail with pink tips high on her head. She blew out a huge puff of air. "I swear all the residents in the county are here for the festival, and none of them thought to get their hair styled before they arrived. It's been a zoo since day one." She snapped her gum.

"It's okay, really. I'll just wait until he's free."

She snorted. "Good luck." Then she went back to answering the phones that had been ringing off the hook since I walked in.

I saw Raoulle across the room, finishing up with a client. I bit my bottom lip and bypassed the receptionist. It was worth a shot. I waved to him and caught his eyes. He held up his hands in a I-need-ten-minutes signal. Ten minutes wasn't bad. I gave him a thumbs up and took a seat in the waiting room. Nearly thirty minutes passed before he finally motioned me over to his chair.

"Oh, thank you so much, Raoulle. I really need to speak with you."

"Honey, if I'm missing my break for you, then you're paying me. Have a seat." He pushed me down into his chair and slung a cape around me, tying it in the back.

"B-But I don't need a haircut." My eyes met his in the mirror.

"B-But you're getting one." He pulled out his comb and scissors and started clipping away.

Oh, Lord, my hair was short already. I wouldn't have much left by the time he was done if I didn't do something quick.

"Start talking, sugar. You've got fifteen minutes before my next client, and my stomach's growling. Don't make me regret this."

"Okay, so you know all the break-ins that happened in town recently?" I started rambling, my thoughts a jumbled mess as I watched strand after pale blond strand fall to the floor.

"Oh, my word, yes. I knew about poor Gary and his hardware store getting trashed. Everyone in town was afraid of the Rebel Riders. Then after the murder, we all thought the gang had left town. But then Granny Gert told me about poor Jo. And then Natalie told me a couple days later when I was giving her highlights—which are the bomb and look amazing on her if I do say so myself—that she and Sam had break-ins at the café and bakery as well. I'm afraid every day when I show up for work at the salon what I might find."

Good Lord, he rambled more than I did. "Well, I don't know if this is public knowledge or not—probably not—so I need you to keep this between you and me." I gave him a no-nonsense warning look straight from a page in Grumpy Pants' book.

"My lips are sealed, honey." Raoulle pretended to turn a key in his mouth and throw it away over his shoulder.

I rolled my eyes and refocused. "There was a blond sample of hair on the floor in the café after the break-in. We all know Natalie is a neat freak, so she definitely wouldn't have closed up shop for the day with that on her floor. It had to have been left behind by whoever broke into her shop."

Raoulle's mouth unhinged, falling wide open. So much for the lock and key. "Now I'm going to look at everyone who has blond hair and shiver."

"Except it wasn't normal blond hair." I lowered my voice. "It was from a wig."

"Well, Balayage my bangs, you don't say?"

"You've been hanging around Granny Gert far too much these days," I said on a chuckle, then grew sober as I pointed at him. "Anyway, remember you're my informant. Mum's the word."

"Oh, the word is mum, sugar. But how am I an informant?"

"Because I need to know who wears a wig in Divinity?"

"First off, informant or not, I will *never* spill my client's personal secrets. Stylist client confidentiality and all that." He tapped the top of my head with his comb. "Shame on you for even asking." His fingers were flying as fast as his words, and my eyes widened as I saw my locks grow shorter and shorter in the mirror.

"Raoulle!" I reached up and grabbed his hand.

He met my horrified gaze in the mirror with an *Oh* forming on his silent lips. "My bad, but honey, you always look cute."

Cute! Not exactly what I was going for in winning my fiancé over into wanting to have my babies. I sighed, pushing that thought from my mind. "No more cutting, please. Just style it. I'm sure it will be fine."

Raoulle put some gel in it, then tried to brush it to the side, to the back... any direction at all. The uneven strands were so short, they bounced straight back up, making me look like a long lost relative of David Bowie.

I swallowed hard and stopped looking at the mess on my head in the mirror. Spinning my chair around, I faced him. "Can you at least tell me who makes wigs in Divinity?"

"Well, that's easy. No one."

I felt my forehead wrinkle.

"But," he held up his finger for me to wait as he grabbed pen and paper and wrote a name and address down, "There's a woman in Stillwater who does a fabulous job. As far as I know, her shop is the only place to get a wig in the entire county."

I took the note and hopped out of my chair. "Thank you, Raoulle. I owe you."

"Good, you can start by tipping me for the haircut."

I looked in the mirror, reaching a hand up toward the chunky strands, then thought better of it as I cringed and met his gaze. "Here's your tip. Don't talk with your hands when cutting someone's hair. I'm beginning to think *you* owe me."

"Touché."

"Remember, mum's the word."

"I will if you will. Don't tell anyone I'm responsible for *that*." He pointed to my head and shuddered, then motioned me away and signaled for his next client to take a seat.

Oh, I wasn't saying a word to anyone. Good thing it was winter, because I had a sudden hankering for a new collection of hats.

15

I pulled my white knit beanie down over my ears and looked in the rear-view mirror of my VW Bug. Thank goodness for hats. It didn't look half bad. In fact, it looked kind of cute, but Lord help me if I had to take it off.

An hour later, I arrived in Stillwater. At least this time the sun was shining bright, and the roads were free of snow. I'd plugged the address Raoulle had given me into my phone and followed the map. It took me to Styles by Renee, a cute little salon in the center of town. I parked by the curb and headed inside. Unlike Pump Up the Volume, this place wasn't busy at all. There was a stylist working on one woman's hair, but the rest of the chairs were vacant.

I walked up to the front desk and smiled at the receptionist. "Hi, I'm Sunny Meadows. I was wondering if Renee Jordan was in?"

Before she could answer, a woman emerged from the back room. She had the most glorious long, curly milk-chocolate brown hair and honey-colored eyes. "I'm Renee, the owner. How can I help you Ms. Meadows?"

"Please, call me Sunny. I heard you make wigs here."

"Why yes we do. Let's see what we're looking at here." Before I realized what she had in mind, she pulled off my beanie.

I gasped, and reflectively raised a hand to my hair.

"Oh. My. Goodness." She looked at me in shock then with pity. "Don't worry, we'll fix you right up, hon."

"No, I don't—"

"Now, there's no shame in losing your hair. Why, I have plenty of women with alopecia who come to me for help. There's always something that can be done. Follow me, my dear." She took my arm and led me to a back room.

My eyes widened. The room was filled with wigs of all colors and styles. A comfortable plush chair sat before a big mirror with lots of lights.

"Have a seat, honey, and we'll get you measured."

"I really don't need a wig. I just wanted to..." My voice trailed off as her expression went from sympathetic and comforting to suspicious.

"Where did you say you were from?" she asked.

"You're right, I do need a wig. I just didn't want to admit I'm losing my hair." I couldn't believe I was mentally thanking Raoulle for giving me bald patches.

Renee relaxed and patted my shoulder. "It's okay. All sorts of things cause hair loss. It doesn't have to mean it's permanent. Have you been under any stress lately?"

Had I ever. "Actually, yes. My fiancé isn't sure he wants children, and I'm not sure if that's a deal breaker or not." I hadn't meant to say that out loud, but it had been on my mind a lot. Sometimes it was easier to talk to a complete stranger.

"Oh, hon, I'm sorry about that." She wrapped a tape measure around my head in several directions and wrote down the sizes. "I had an almost-fiancé once. I really thought he was the one, but then he dumped me for some floozy." She pursed her lips before continuing, "The woman was married. What could possibly come of that? Life is so unfair sometimes." She headed over to the wall and searched through a section of wigs.

"Now I'm the one who's sorry. That must have been awful."

"It was. I tried to forget about him, but I couldn't stop loving him. He was always such a take-charge kind of man. I admired that about him, but he hung around with another guy I didn't particularly care for. I think his friend was a bad influence. But when we were together, he was his true self. And now I'll never have the chance to show him how much I cared even after all of the bad things he did." She came back with a short brown wig and tried it on my head. "How's that?"

"But I have blond hair?"

She reached her hand up to her hairline then pulled her hair clean off. "So do I." Her blond hair was a dirty blond color and pinned up so it wouldn't show through. She slipped the glorious wig back on. "Sometimes it's fun to mix things up a bit."

"Hmmm, I never thought of that." I turned my head from side to side, reveling in the difference a simple color change meant. I looked like a totally different person. Except I wasn't here to switch things up. I was here to discover who in Divinity wore one of her blond wigs, or possibly, if she did. "Um, I think I'll stick with my original color. At least for now. Baby steps and all that." I smiled a little.

"Gotcha." She went back to the wall of wigs.

"Do you get many requests for blond wigs?" I tried to sound casual.

She stopped what she was doing and looked off in the distance for a moment before continuing. "We get requests for all sorts of wigs. Drag queens, alopecia clients, cancer patients, or simply bored housewives. Why do you ask?"

"Well, I'm from Divinity, and—"

Renee tripped and dropped the wig she was holding. "Sorry, you were saying?" Her eyes had narrowed considerably as she walked back over behind me, her face looking suddenly flushed.

Our gazes met in the mirror. "Well, you probably know that Winterfest is going on. I saw this really pretty shade of blond from a distance. I thought maybe it was a wig, but I couldn't quite tell. I asked my hair stylist, Raoulle at Pump Up the Volume, and he said they don't make wigs in Divinity. He gave me your name and shop, and said you did fabulous work."

Renee relaxed slightly, then slid the wig on my head. "You can't tell my wigs aren't the real deal," she said with pride. "But I haven't sold a blond wig or any other color to anyone in Divinity."

"Oh." I couldn't hide the disappointment from my voice. "I was hoping to replicate that particular wig."

"I'm sure we can find one you'll like. Oh, wait right here. I just remembered something." She headed into another storage room and emerged moments later with a blond wig that had my heartrate speeding up.

It was the same color as the hair sample from the café.

"I think that's it!" I sat up straighter.

"I didn't sell this wig in Divinity. I sold it to Nancy Culligan. She lives here in Stillwater. Poor thing has breast cancer. She beat it, thank the Lord, but her hair hasn't grown back in yet. I made her one when she first got cancer, but she lost it. How on earth you lose a wig is beyond me, but I was able to make her another one the same color as the first one. Except, she wanted this one longer. This here's a backup, just in case. I took it for a test drive, and no one was the wiser. Now that her hair is growing back, I'm sure it would be okay if you took this one."

Interesting. I wondered just where that test drive she'd taken had been. "Have you ever been to Divinity?"

"Just once recently." A sad expression crossed over her face for a moment, and she visibly blinked back what appeared to be genuine tears. "After a funeral."

"Oh, I'm so terribly sorry. Who died?"

She looked me square in the eye as she responded, "My almost-fiancé."

"Um, dare I ask?" Mitch looked up from our kitchen table. He was eating a sandwich. I'd been gone all morning and hadn't expected to run into him.

"Oh, you're home. I didn't think I would see you until dinner."

"Why, got a hot date, Natasha?"

I wrinkled up my nose at him. "What are you talking about?"

He pointed to my head. "You look like a Russian spy." Then he took another bite of his sandwich.

I reached my hand up and laughed. "I forgot I was wearing this." I pulled the long blond wig off.

"Ah, that explains a lot." He studied my chopped

hair and then squinted. "Actually, no, it doesn't. Looks like you had an eventful morning."

I felt the heat rush to my cheeks. "Whoops, I definitely forgot about my new haircut. I know, it looks awful."

"I'd call it a mid-life crisis, but you're too young for that." His gaze softened. "You couldn't look awful if you tried, but would you care to explain?"

My insides warmed. No matter what, my grumpy detective always made me feel beautiful and loved. That had never been our problem. Aligning our future goals was the elephant in the room. I bit back a sigh and responded, "Actually, yes, I will definitely respond. But first," I slid his plate in front of me, "I'm starved."

His lips twitched but he didn't move to stop me as I dug in with relish, closing my eyes as I chewed. He chuckled, then I heard him slide his chair back and make another sandwich. We both knew I couldn't do much more than boil water for my tea.

I opened my eyes. "Thank you. And, Mitch?" I waited until his eyes met mine. "I love you."

He stared at me for a long moment, then sat down to join me. "I know. Ditto, babe."

"I really am sorry for scaring you the other day."

He nodded once. "Apology accepted. And I'm sorry for shutting you out. I'm working on that."

"I know, and I appreciate that. And for the record I'm impulsive, yes, but I try not to be reckless. We're a team. You have to start treating me like an equal and stop trying to protect me from the world."

"I only do that because it would kill me if anything bad ever happened to you." He reached out and squeezed my hand. "I can't even think about what my life would be like if I lost you." We were suddenly talking about more than the snowmobile race with me following Ray.

"I know," I answered the first part of his response, but left the second part lingering. I couldn't promise him forever if we couldn't come to terms on what we wanted our future to look like. I wanted children, he didn't seem to. I could compromise on having just one, but I didn't think I could live without any. The question was, could I live without him? I couldn't imagine that either, so I turned the conversation to a less troubling topic.

"So, I got my hair cut today."

A loud laugh burst out of Mitch's chest, and I couldn't help smiling in return.

"Is that what you're calling it?"

"I had free time on my hands today, but a certain detective didn't want to bring me with him to see Captain Walker. So, I went to the café and drank some tea."

"What the heck was in that tea to possess you to get your hair cut like that?"

"Blond hair."

His lips parted, and his confused expression was priceless.

"I ran into Nancy. She told me that the blond hair from the crime scene was from a wig."

He was already nodding. "Pretty much what Captain Walker told me."

"That's where the hair butchering comes in. I went to see Raoulle at the salon, but the place was packed. He refused to talk to me unless I got a haircut from him."

Mitch drew his jet-black brows into a deep V. "Remind me never to get a haircut from him again."

"No kidding. That man gives a new meaning to the

expression 'talk with your hands.' Not a very smart thing to do when holding a pair of scissors. Anyway, I learned from Raoulle that the only place to buy a wig is in Stillwater."

"Ah, I'm guessing that's where that wig you had on comes into play?"

"Exactly. I went to see Renee Jordan at Styles by Renee in Stillwater." I waited for the lecture and was surprised when I didn't get one.

He read my expression correctly and responded, "I'm trying."

"And I thank you for that." I leaned over and kissed his cheek. "Renee said the only blond wig she has sold recently belongs to a cancer patient named Nancy Culligan who lives in Stillwater. The biggest thing I learned is that Renee Jordan was Gunther Corp's ex-girlfriend."

"I know."

"You do?" I should have known. It was hard to surprise my detective. He was very good at his job.

"I talked to Juan as soon as I left Captain Walker's office."

"Renee did say she was in Divinity for Gunther's funeral. She also admitted to taking the wig for a test drive, but she didn't say where. Maybe she wore the wig when she came to Divinity and broke into the businesses to try to frame the Rebel Riders. She said her boyfriend dumped her for a married woman. She also made it clear she hated his right-hand man. I'm taking that to mean Ray. Although, she claims she hasn't been back to Divinity since, but she could be lying."

"You might be right. She very well could be behind the break-ins. I'll have to look into that more. Thank you. Good work, Tink."

My chest swelled with pride. "You're welcome, Detective." My heart warmed.

Progress.

"So, what are your plans right now? I still have half
an hour before I have to get back to work."

"Nothing why?"

"Follow me, Natasha," his gaze ran over every inch
of me and heated as he added, "and grab your wig."

For the first time, I didn't argue and did exactly as I
was told.

LATER THAT NIGHT, DETECTIVE STONE AND I HEADED
to Divine Inspiration for dinner. The inn was pretty
full with the overflow from the festival staying there.
My father and Henry were in their glory, telling stories
by the fire, dressed in slacks and cozy sweaters. They
had half a circle of guests giving them their undivided
attention in the living room. Great-Grandma Tootsie,
Granny Gert, and Fiona were hard at work in the
kitchen preparing dinner, while my mother fretted
about, double-checking everything with Sally Clark
the housekeeper, who was my mother's sanity. The
woman ran the inn like a well-oiled machine, and was
the only competent employee other than Toots that
my mother had.

Her words, not mine.

"What can I do, Mother?" I asked, feeling the need
to at least pretend to help.

"Enjoy yourself, my darling. We've got everything
under control." She stood ramrod straight with perfect
posture, impeccably dressed. "Don't we, Ms. Clark?"

Sally nodded sharply, then gave me a wink the
second my mother looked away. I mouthed a *thank you*

to her, then breathed the first sigh of relief I'd felt all week. At least something was going right. I was worried we were running into dead ends on all our leads. There was no way to prove that Ray or Kristen had killed Gunther.

The same went for Renee. She might have been in Divinity, but if she wore a wig, then no one would be able to point her out in a lineup. She said she was there for the funeral, that's it. There was no way to prove she was there before and killed Gunther, or that she came back later to do the break-ins and frame the Rebel Riders.

That was why Mitch and I had chosen to eat with my parents tonight. Neither one of us could bear to face Jo and Cole without any more encouraging news. And we really did feel bad about not being able to help my parents more on their new endeavor, with the investigation still going on.

Granny Gert came out of the kitchen to announce that dinner was ready and would be served in the dining room. We all headed to that room and took our seats.

"Sunshine Meadows, where are your manners?" my mother asked me in front of everyone, shaking her head and tsking.

I felt the heat hit my ears this time. "Um, I'm not sure what you mean, Mother?" I folded my hands, prepared to say grace.

My father tapped his head, and I stifled a groan.

Great. This day just kept getting better and better. I slowly reached up and pulled off my white beanie.

"Boys oh day, what happened to your hair, child?" Great-Grandma Tootsie asked, and nearly dropped the rack of lamb. Ralph quickly grabbed the tray from her, staying by her side to make sure she didn't faint straight away.

"Oh, my word," Fiona sputtered. "These kids and their crazy styles these days."

"Land sake's, child, that's one fad I will *not* be following." Granny Gert patted her perfectly styled snow-white curls.

"Are you truly trying to give me a heart attack?" my mother sputtered.

Just then the doorbell rang.

"I'll get it!" I shouted, and took off for the front door. Saved by the bell.

I opened the door without looking through the peephole, then gasped at the sight before me. Kristen Peters stood there with tears streaming down her face.

"I need to see my husband, please."

Well, at least the attention will be off of me, was all I could think as I led the way into the dining room. All heck broke loose at that point.

The giant known as Ralph barked, "What the hell are you doing here?"

16

The minute that Ralph realized Kristen was crying, his entire demeanor had changed. Even after all she'd put him through, he obviously still loved her. They'd been talking in the library for the past hour while we finished dinner and cleaned up. None of the guests knew what was going on, but the rest of us did. Everyone dispersed, retiring to their rooms, while the rest of us congregated in the living room, waiting.

"What on earth do you think this is about?" my father asked.

"Nothing good if you ask me," my mother responded. "We don't need any more drama around here." She eyed my hair.

I slid my knit hat back on.

"Nonsense," Granny Gert chimed in. "You know what they say about publicity. Even negative publicity is a good thing."

"That's true," Fiona added. "At least people will be talking about the inn."

"All I know is that poor man has been through enough." Great-Grandma Tootsie added her two cents.

"He's just a big ole' teddy bear. I'd hate to see him get hurt again."

The door to the library opened, and Ralph came out holding Kristen's hand. "My wife would like to stay here if that's all right with you." He looked at my mother.

"We're fully booked." My mother eyed Kristen warily.

He pulled Kristen closer. "She'll be staying with me."

"Well, that's settled then. I'll get some tea." Toots headed to the kitchen, humming show tunes all the way.

Detective Stone pulled out his notebook and looked at Kristen. "You mind if I ask you some questions?"

"She's been through enough for one night," Ralph grumbled.

"It's okay. I want to talk to the detective." Kristen squeezed her husband's hand, then let go and sat in a chair in the living room.

Mitch took a seat on the couch across from her, and I sat beside him. He looked around the room and raised an eyebrow, waiting. Everyone else took the hint and left the room.

Scanning his notes, Mitch said, "Last time I talked to you, you said you were afraid of your husband." He looked up at the giant. "No offense."

Ralph remained silent.

"I was afraid of him because he was so angry when he found out about my affair with Gunther."

"Renee Jordan was the one who tipped me off," Ralph added. "She was pretty upset, and took the breakup hard."

Mitch and I glanced at each other. Hard enough to

kill over? We filed that tidbit away, then focused back on Ralph.

"I was angry. My wife had every right to be afraid of me then, even though I would never actually hurt her. But I'm different now. I understand I played a role in our problems. I wasn't around much." He dropped his gaze to the floor. "I wasn't a very good husband."

"I don't blame you for being angry with me." Kristen reached out and took his hand in hers. "I never should have turned to someone else. I should have just talked to you."

"You said Ray Simone was a friend of yours. That you were staying with him for your safety. Why did that change? Do you no longer feel safe with him?" I asked, pulling out my own notebook and jotting down notes.

Detective Stone's lips tipped up just a hair as he glanced at my notebook, but he didn't dare make a comment.

"I thought Ray was a friend," Kristen said, "but he wasn't." She shivered. "He's always been jealous of Gunther. He has wanted to be the leader of the Rebel Riders for years. Now that Gunther is gone, Ray is letting the power trip get to his head. Wayne Emerson wasn't the violent one. Yes, he made a pass at me, but Ray was the one who went crazy smashing the wood."

I knew there had been something off about him. I jotted notes in my book.

"Why did you lie about that before?" Mitch looked up from his own.

She inhaled a shaky breath. "Because I knew if I said the truth, Ray would hurt me without thinking twice." Ralph squeezed her hand.

"Who was the other woman at the cabin?" I asked. "I didn't recognize her. She looked... *fancy*."

"I don't know who she is. Ray has many women who visit him. I asked him about it once, and he told me to mind my own business. So that's what I did. There are a ton of people from towns all over who come to the festival. She could be from anywhere." Kristen rubbed her temple. "Although, come to think of it, I haven't seen her around since the day of the race."

"Did you lie about the Rebel Riders, too? Are they the ones behind the break-ins?" Mitch watched her closely.

Kristen was already shaking her head. "Honestly, I haven't seen the gang around at all since Gunther died. That's another thing that's making Ray come unhinged. The gang doesn't take him seriously like they did Gunther. I think they've moved on without him."

"So, if strong-arming businesses for protection is a thing of the past, then what's Ray's next plan?"

"I don't know. You'll have to ask him." She let go of Ralph's hand and twisted hers in her lap. Mitch remained silent, just studying her. "I'm tired now. Can we be done?" She looked up at Ralph. "I'd like to go to our room."

"Yeah, we're done." He gave Mitch a hard stare, then helped Kristen to her feet and showed her to their room.

Great-Grandma Tootsie came out of the kitchen with a steaming pot of tea and several mugs. She looked around the room. "Oh, the poor dear must have been worn out. Anyone else care for tea?"

Worn out and lying through her teeth, I thought. Ray was up to something, all right, but Kristen was too afraid to say what. Afraid enough to return to her husband after cheating on him. The question was what exactly was he up to? Nothing like a cup of tea to help me ponder. "Thank you, Toots. I'd love some tea."

"How about you, Detective?" Toots asked.

"I'll take a raincheck." His gaze met mine. "There's somewhere I have to be, and it might take all night. Don't wait up." His gaze pleaded with me for understanding, and I nodded once. Duty called, and I had some thinking of my own to do.

———

IT WAS THE MIDDLE OF THE NIGHT. I WAS TOSSING AND turning with the worst feeling in my gut. I'd been having bad dreams all night but couldn't seem to remember the details. Everything was fuzzy. My head felt all spacy. Maybe I was coming down with a cold. Something pounced on my chest. I gasped and bolted straight up to a sitting position.

Morty.

I let out a huge sigh of relief, then scowled at my cat. He was so white in the darkness, he almost appeared to be glowing.

"Morty Meadows, you'd better have a good explanation for scaring me half to death." He climbed off my chest.

I glanced to the side of our bed, but Mitch was still gone. I frowned. He hadn't been kidding when he said he might be gone all night. I trusted him completely. I just hoped he was safe. Morty usually only acted this way when he was trying to tell me something.

I flipped back the covers and climbed out of bed. That's when I noticed he was standing on a piece of paper. I lifted him off the paper and picked it up. The flyer for Divine Inspiration. That was weird.

I headed downstairs to the kitchen to make

some cocoa. Maybe that would help me sleep. When I got to the kitchen, Morty was standing on the counter. It still amazed me that I never saw him eat or sleep, and he moved at lightning speed, too fast for the human eye to see. One minute he was upstairs, the next he beat me to the kitchen.

I tried to walk past him, but he scratched at the paper beneath his paws. I looked at what he stood on. The flyer for Divine Inspiration again. What was going on at the hotel that needed my attention in the middle of the night?

He stared at me.

"Okay, buddy, you've got my attention. You feel it too, don't you?"

He meowed.

I stood there for a minute, thinking.

He meowed louder.

"Okay, okay." I headed back upstairs to get dressed. My mother was going to kill me if I woke her up for nothing.

Fifteen minutes later, I pulled into the parking lot of Divine Inspiration and cut the engine to my Bug. I searched the area, but didn't see anything amiss. The inn was packed with cars and all the rooms were full. I got out and headed inside. Harry was manning the front desk.

"Sunny? What on earth are you doing here? It's four in the morning."

"I know. I couldn't sleep." I tightened my coat around me. "Bad dreams."

"Do you want me to get Vivian?"

"No, no. Please don't." I glanced around the quiet inn. "You haven't seen anything weird tonight, have you?"

"Have you seen the crew we live with?" He chuckled. "Define weird."

"True." I laughed. "Okay, suspicious, then."

He pushed his glasses up his nose. "No, can't say that I have."

"I'm beginning to think my cat is crazy."

"Your cat?"

"Don't ask." I massaged my temples because my head still felt fuzzy. I turned around to leave, and there stood Morty.

"Now *that's* weird," Harry said. "But I've stopped questioning the comings and goings of that one." He pointed at my cat with his pen.

"Same."

Morty ran past me and headed up the stairs. Something told me to follow. I kept my distance and stayed in the shadows. At the top of the stairs, I followed Morty down a hallway to an open door. Peeking into the room, I saw a giant shadow lying on the bed. I was so embarrassed. This was Ralph Peters' room. There was no mistaking that shadow. I was about to leave, but I heard a moan. For some reason, my senses came alert. That moan didn't sound normal.

Taking a chance that I was right, I entered the room and walked over to the side of the bed. Ralph lay there in an unconscious heap. I shook his shoulder, but he didn't stir. I felt his head, but he didn't have a fever. I shook his arm harder, but nothing. Turning on the light, I lifted his eyelids and studied his pupils. Just as I thought. He'd been drugged. That's why my head felt fuzzy. I'd somehow picked up a reading. I tapped both sides of his face.

"Mr. Peters, wake up."

Nothing.

I tapped harder. "Ralph. Can you hear me?"

Nothing.

That's when I noticed the other side of the bed was empty.

I ran to the window, which I now saw was open, and looked down below. I didn't see anything. I searched harder, and finally saw, by the edge of the river out back, there was a flash of a white. It was different than Morty. It almost looked like a nightgown.

Kristen!

I couldn't wait for backup. The first day or two were crucial in a kidnapping. Everyone knew that, right? Or had I been watching too many crime shows? Either way, I wasn't taking any chances. I opened the window wider and climbed out onto the ledge. My parents hadn't put the screens in yet. That would happen in the spring. The cold temperatures had turned everything to ice. My feet kept slipping with every step I took. Oh, Lord, if I came out of this in one piece, I would never do anything impulsive again.

With the next step I took, my feet slipped off the ledge completely. I dangled by my fingertips for a few moments, but I knew it wouldn't last. I swallowed my scream when they gave way. My arms flailed in every direction until somehow, someway, I came into contact with a branch and latched on instinctively.

My body jerked to a stop. I dangled there, trying to catch my breath, but it didn't last long. The brittle branch broke in half and down I went. Thank goodness it was winter. I landed in a heaping pile of snow. I squirmed about until I finally found my footing, and then I climbed out of the snowbank that had saved my life. As fast as my boots could carry me, I headed to the river. I was worried I was too late, but when I reached the edge of the river, my father was there. He stood guard over a knocked-out

Kristen, with his fishing pole at the ready like a sword.

"Dad, what are you doing out here?"

"I was getting ready for the ice fishing competition today when I saw a dark form carrying a woman dressed in a white nightgown. I didn't know who it was, but I knew something was wrong. Who would carry a woman dressed only in a nightgown over their shoulder? So, I grabbed one of my poles and chased after them, shouting for the person to stop. The figure seemed surprised to see anyone out here that time of night, so they dropped the woman and took off into the woods. By the time I got here, I was surprised to see Mrs. Peters. Your mother will say 'I told you so' over this one. She was worried that letting her stay at the inn would cause drama."

"That's an understatement."

"Why are *you* here, is the question I want to know?"

"Well, it started with a nightmare. Then Morty jumped on my chest. Then there was the flyer for the inn. Then I found Ralph Peters drugged in his bed. And Kristen was missing. Then there's the matter that I almost died. Thank goodness for the snowbank that broke my fall out of the second story window."

My dad rubbed his forehead. "I'm almost sorry I asked."

A moan came from on the ground, so my father and I knelt down beside Kristen.

"Mrs. Peters?" I asked.

Nothing.

"Kristen? Can you hear me?"

A slight mumbled, "Yes," came out of her lips.

I breathed a sigh of relief. "This is Sunny. You've

had a little mishap. We're going to bring you back to the inn now."

"She'll be okay. The first thing I did was check her vitals."

My father might be retired, but the doctor in him would always emerge when needed. And while he might be getting on in years, but he was still plenty strong enough. He picked Kristen up and carried her as we made our way back to the inn. By now, everyone was up. There would be questions. And hopefully, we would finally get some answers.

17

"I just knew she would be trouble." My mother fussed about the inn hours later as she got ready for the ice fishing competition reception.

My father and Harry were running the fishing part with the maintenance man's guidance, while my mother readied the inn with her housekeeper's help. Meanwhile, Great-Grandma Tootsie, Granny Gert, and Fiona prepared the food for the celebration after the competition was over. Everyone had worked so hard to pull off opening the inn early. It amazed me how quickly it had all come together, but I shouldn't be surprised really. My parents were both hard working individuals, used to being successful at whatever they wanted to do.

"Well, you don't have much choice in letting her stay here, Mother," I responded. "She is Ralph Peters' wife, after all."

Kristen had been drugged, same as Ralph. She didn't remember a thing, let alone who had taken her. Ralph came out from under the influence of the drugs, and the teddy bear turned into a grizzly once he heard about what had happened. He was positive it was Ray who had taken Kristen. While she went back to bed to sleep off the drugs and the trauma of nearly being kidnapped, Ralph had taken off for parts unknown. Now it was hours later, half the town had arrived for the competition, and I had yet to hear from my favorite detective.

"Hopefully, she'll sleep all afternoon and stay out of the way." My mother rearranged a centerpiece on the dining room table three times.

"Have some pity, Mother. That was quite a trauma she went through. At least it happened in the middle of the night before everyone got here."

"If you ask me, she brought it on herself, trolloping about with another man in the middle of the night while still married."

"That's not for us to judge. Either way, it had to be scary. Thank goodness Dad was there to save the day."

"Ah, yes, your father. Mr. Fantastic and his fishing pole, off to save the day one cast at a time. I'll never hear the end of it." She moved on to straightening the throw pillows on the couch. "Donald doesn't have a clue what he's doing out there in that shanty, any more than Harry the Hero sidekick does. The Wonder Twins are going to be the death of me yet. Mark my words." A crash came from the kitchen followed by arguing. "That is if The Tasty Trio doesn't do me in first."

I silently giggled over the nicknames I'd given them. Somehow the Wonder Twins and The Tasty Trio had stuck. "It'll be okay, Mom. You'll see. Everything will be perfect, I'm sure. I mean, what else can possibly go wrong?"

She just stared at me.

"Alrighty then, I think I'll go check out the ice fishing competition. Holler if you need me." I hurried outside and made my way through the crowd to the river. I had to admit I was impressed. My father, Harry, and Frank had rigged up several shanties all over the frozen river. Perfectly cut holes with ice augers were in the center of each one, with chairs and fishing poles surrounding them, and buckets waiting for fish. The men had organized teams for each shanty. The sun was shining, and it didn't feel too cold out this morning.

A perfect day.

"Hey, guys, any bites?" I asked Jo, Cole, Sean, and Zoe as I popped my head into one shanty.

"I haven't caught anything yet." Zoe lifted her pole to check that her bait was still attached to the hook on her line.

"Don't worry, darlin', you will." Sean slung his arm around her shoulders.

"Yeah, well, the bait must not be very good." Cole added more to his pole and dropped it back into the hole.

"The bait is just fine. Look at the size of the fish I caught." A beaming smile spread across Jo's face.

I looked in her bucket and pressed my lips together to stop from laughing. Her fish were twice the size of Cole's. "You can't have the biggest of everything, Sasquatch." I blew him a kiss.

He grunted.

I left and scanned the area but still didn't see Mitch. Making my way back to the shore by my father and Harry, I pulled up a chair around the fire they had proudly started—with Frank's help, of course.

"Nicely done, you two." I put my toes closer to the heat of the fire. I'd been in such a hurry to follow Morty's lead, I'd neglected to put on my wool socks.

My father puffed up his chest. "Thank you, Sunny. I was a bit worried after this morning's rough start, but

I think we pulled off a pretty good competition." He glanced around at the fairly large crowd in attendance.

"I would have to agree," Harry seconded. "I guess word of the kidnapping attempt hasn't gotten around yet. Must be Detective Stone is on the job and keeping it quiet.

"Even if it had," Dad chimed in, adding, "I would imagine people would show up out of sheer curiosity."

"Most people do love a good drama," Harry concluded with a firm nod.

"That's very true." I had perked up at the mention of my fiancé, and searched the area again, hoping to see him all safe and sound. "I for one could do without any more drama. I'm just glad you guys had time to finish the setup for the competition."

"It might have taken us all night, but who needs sleep? Right, Donald? We'll be doing plenty of that when we're six feet under."

"Amen to that, Harry. Amen to that. In the meantime, we still have a lot to finish on our bucket list."

"Yes, we do, my boy. Yes, we do." Harry elbowed my father and snickered. "Just don't tell our wives."

I rolled my eyes and warmed my hands by the fire. "Have either of you seen Detective Stone yet today?"

They shook their heads 'no.'

"Well, I'm sure he'll be along soon," I said, more for my own benefit, and pulled my beanie farther down over my ears. My detective could handle himself, of that I was sure. "In the meantime, it looks like you've got quite the competition going. Jo's killing it. I saw some really big fish out there."

"That's true." Frank pulled up a chair to join us. "It won't be long before someone has the catch of the day."

"I got a bite," a woman screamed from inside one of the shanties. "Oh, wow, I think it's a big one."

Several people left their shanties and came running. We followed suit until we made it to the shanty closest to the shore. People were eager to see. I managed to get close enough to peek inside.

Cathy was beaming. "It feels like a huge fish." The line grew slack on her fishing pole. "Oh, no, I think it's getting away."

Zack dropped his pole and jumped up to stand behind her and help hold the rod with his good hand. "Keep reeling it in. I think this could be the winner."

"Pull hard on the line." Miles joined them on Cathy's other side to help. "Don't let it get away. Wait, you've got it. I think I see it. It's... it's..."

Cathy screamed and fainted dead away.

Zack dropped the pole and took several staggering steps backward, gagging.

Miles held steadfast as a grim expression crossed his face.

"Well?" my father asked. "Is it the winner or not? Pull it up through the hole, young man. What kind of fish is it?"

"It's the winner, all right." Miles looked up at us. "But it's not a fish. It's not a what, it's a who."

"E-Excuse me?" I stuttered.

Miles took a deep breath and clarified, "It's a dead body."

MITCH LOOKED OUT THE WINDOWS OF THE SUNROOM overlooking the grounds with his back to everyone that afternoon. We'd had to clear the people from their shanties and end the competition early. The police were called in and the crime scene investigators worked furiously to secure the scene and cut a bigger hole in the ice to extract the body.

What else could possibly happen? I had asked earlier.

Apparently, plenty could still happen. I'd just never expected for someone else to wind up dead, and at the inn, no less. My mother was having the vapors, the Tasty Trio were twittering about in a frenzy of chaos, and the Wonder Twins were at a loss as to how to fix everything. I, for one, was glad to have my Grumpy Pants back.

"Ray Simone isn't just dead. The coroner said he died from strangulation, not drowning." My fiancé turned around to face the room, Detective Stone firmly in place. "Looks like we have another murder on our hands."

"It wasn't me; I swear it." Ralph waved his hands in front of him and backed up a step or two, looking around as if for the nearest exit.

Mitch eyed him as he unbuttoned his jacket, revealing his side arm. "Where were you after the attempted kidnapping of your wife until you returned just now?"

"I needed to clear my head. I know how it looks. I'll admit I tried to find Ray to talk to him, but he wasn't anywhere."

"Did you stop for breakfast or go to a store? Anything where someone can corroborate your whereabouts?" I asked.

Ralph shook his head, his long beard swinging. "I knew I wouldn't be good company for anyone until I cooled off, but I promise you I would never kill anyone."

"That's true." Kristen moved closer to him. "He really is all bark and no bite. He wouldn't harm anyone."

"That's not what you said when you went into hiding with Ray not that long ago," I added. "You said you were afraid of him."

"I was afraid because I had never seen him so angry, but deep down I knew he wouldn't hurt me."

"I heard you say 'I'll kill him' after your wife returned bruised and drugged," Sally Clark pointed out.

"Yeah, I told you trying to find Mr. Simone was a bad idea," Frank added with a grim expression on his face, "but you wouldn't listen."

"That doesn't mean I'm a killer." Ralph looked around the room so helplessly, I was inclined to believe him.

"Boys oh day, we believe you're innocent, Ralph." Great-Grandma Tootsie patted his shoulder.

"Oh, fiddlesticks, everyone here knows you're just a big ole teddy bear." Granny Gert stood on his other side.

Fiona came up behind him and looked over his head at everyone in the room. "This poor man has been through enough." Her gaze landed on his wife briefly before settling on the detective. "He has been nothing but helpful around here, and more forgiving than he should be, if you ask me. I believe he's innocent."

My mother harrumphed but didn't say a word after my father shot her a warning look.

Harry, the former judge, seconded his wife. "I might be old, but I'm a good judge of character, and I say innocent until proven guilty. Hear, hear."

"Good luck with that," Jo said, adjusting her enormous belly. Cole put his arm around her but didn't offer any words of encouragement, because she was right. Someone was desperately trying to frame him for a murder he didn't commit, and his own good character hadn't seemed to matter much. We were running out of time to prove otherwise.

"None of you know what it was like, reeling in a dead body. I can still see his bloated face staring up at me through the ice hole. I just know I'm going to have nightmares for years." Cathy shuddered. "I don't think I'll ever be the same."

Zack shivered, and Morty appeared from the corner of the room. He jumped on Zack's lap, and Zack calmed instantly.

"It doesn't matter what any of us think," Miles chimed in. "If the clues point to a suspect, it makes it pretty hard to ignore that." He glanced at Cole with a wince, then let his gaze settle on Ralph with a frown.

"How do we know Ray didn't kill Gunther, and then someone else, who Ray had a beef with, took him out?" Sean asked.

"We *don't* know that," Mitch answered. "Ray had plenty of enemies, even in his own gang. According to my buddy, Detective Torres, they didn't want him to replace Gunther as their leader. His killer could be anyone."

"Well, all I know is that it's not me," Ralph said.

The Tasty Trio started consoling him, and everyone else started talking about what to do about the ice fishing competition being cancelled and if the rest of Winterfest would continue. The mayor did not want any more events cancelled. The town counted on the money the festival brought in, but murder was a little different than an attempted kidnapping. There would be no keeping this quiet, especially since half the town had been at the inn for the ice fishing competition. Could we risk someone else being murdered?

"What if Ray wasn't the person who tried to

kidnap me?" Kristen rubbed her arms. "What if that person killed Ray and is still after me?"

"I'll protect you." Ralph put his arm around her.

Mitch stared him down. "Isn't that what got you into trouble now?"

"Legally," Ralph clarified. "I'll protect her legally."

"See that you do," Mitch responded. "I've got enough matters to look into. I don't need to be worrying about what crazy thing you might do next."

"He'll behave. You have my word," Kristen said. "We both will." They huddled together, speaking in low tones to each other.

I joined Mitch by the window. "I almost forgot to ask you. Did that lead you were following in Stillwater pan out?" He'd been gone all night, and had just come from briefing Captain Walker when the call came in over the police scanner about the discovery of a dead body beneath the ice.

"Actually, yes." He glanced around the room, but everyone had fallen into their own conversations. He motioned for me to follow him out of the sunroom. We wandered out of earshot and into the living room, but no one really noticed.

"Why all the secrecy?"

"The investigation for Gunther's death is ongoing, and there are still suspects in that room. The intel is on a need-to-know basis, and they don't need to know."

A warmth spread through me over my detective finally realizing we made a good team and acknowledging I needed to know. I crossed my arms and waited patiently.

He glanced around until he was sure we were alone. "Remember when Renee Jordan said she sold a blond wig to Nancy Culligan, the woman from Stillwater who had cancer?"

"Yes, and she lost her first wig so Renee made her a second one that was longer. The long blond one she gave me."

"That's right. Did you know Nancy is married?"

"No, why does that matter?"

"Culligan is her married name."

"And...?"

"So, guess what her maiden name is."

"I have no clue, Mitch. What are you getting at?" He was being more dramatic than the lead in a Broadway musical.

"Nancy Culligan is Nancy Burrows."

"As in..."

"That's right. Nancy is Adam Burrows' sister."

18

The next several hours were spent out by the river at the crime scene. The grounds were deserted and the wind had picked up, bringing a chill to the air. Mayor Cromwell, Chief Spencer, Captain Walker, Detective Fuller, and Mitch had all been discussing Ray Simone's death, as well as Gunther Corp's, and what, if anything, they had in common.

"This is exactly what I didn't want to happen." The mayor shook his oversized troll head as he paced the ice by the shanty where the dead body was caught. "The whole day is shot, which means revenue loss for the town."

Mitch's lookalike, Chief Spencer, was nodding. "Corp's case should have already been wrapped up." He glared at me as if it were *my* fault.

"I think we've made a lot of progress in ruling out the *wrong* suspects, wouldn't you agree, Detective Stone?" I stared my fiancé down, waiting to see whose side he would take. I wasn't about to let Cole take the fall for a crime he didn't commit just for the sake of the town's festival. An innocent man's future was at stake.

"You're right, Ms. Meadows. We have made a fair amount of progress so we can be sure to put away the right person." He glanced at me, then quickly looked at the chief. "I think we're getting close, Chief. I don't know if Corp and Simone's murders had anything to do with each other, but we do have a new lead to follow."

"I'm listening." Chief Spencer crossed his arms over his chest and waited.

Detective Torres arrived at that moment, right on cue. A tall woman with olive skin and curly brown hair walked beside him.

"Hey, Chief," Juan said.

"Torres." Chief Spencer nodded once.

"I'd like you to meet a friend of mine. This is Lindsey Fontanna. She's a dancer at a club in Stillwater." Juan faced the woman. "It's okay, Lindsey. Why don't you tell the gentlemen what you told me?"

She took a deep breath and looked around at all the men, her gaze finally settling on me. She let the air out on a slow exhale and relaxed her shoulders. "My friend Jasmine Jackson and I used to dance together a long time ago. She's a single mom. Dancing isn't enough to pay the bills, you know?"

I nodded, keeping my eyes locked onto hers and silently encouraging her to keep talking. It was as if we were the only two people there.

"I didn't blame her when she started escorting sugar daddies around town. These rich older men who had money to burn but were lonely started paying her to keep them company. It wasn't a physical relationship. They simply needed someone to accompany them to different business functions, charity events, or even just to eat dinner with. In return, they paid her in favors. Paid her rent, bought her clothes, paid her bills, etc."

"Wasn't she afraid of falling victim to sex trafficking?" I asked.

"No, there's a website where you post a profile, and the men select who they are interested in. Then they meet for coffee in a public place and decide if they are a good fit for each other, based on their needs."

"So, what does this have to do with Ray Simone's murder?"

"Jasmine has a daughter. She doesn't normally take any risky chances. She never meets men who aren't through the sugar daddy website. One of her clients, who is the owner of a pretty successful restaurant in Stillwater, referred her to Ray, promising he was legitimate. Jasmine made an exception just this once. She said he was younger than her normal client and better looking. I told her not to, that I had a bad feeling, but she didn't listen. Now, she hasn't been seen or heard from since."

"What did she look like?" I asked.

Lindsey described the woman I had seen with Ray at the cabin in the woods during the snowmobile race.

"Thank you, Lindsey. Detective Stone and I appreciate your help." I reached out and squeezed her hand. "I promise you we will do everything we can to find her."

She sniffed back tears. "Thank you. I'm really worried about her. I'm taking care of her daughter for now, but the poor thing misses her mother."

"Have you been in touch with Jasmine's family?"

"Not yet. I'm hoping I won't have to have that conversation."

Torres finished talking with the men, then escorted Lindsey back to his undercover car and they headed back to Stillwater.

"Good work, Sunny," Captain Walker said.

"Thank you, sir." I smiled, then shot a glance at Chief Spencer, who raised a brow at me but didn't say a word.

"Torres said the restaurant the client owned was under the *protection* of the Rebel Riders. Ray wanted Jasmine, so the client made it happen. End of story." Mitch looked through his notes. The question is... why did Ray want her?"

We heard a rustle from behind us. Turning around, we saw Kristen Peters walking at a fast pace back towards the inn. I looked at Mitch and no words were necessary. We hurried after her and caught up to her before she could walk through the front door.

"Hey," Mitch said in a firm, no-nonsense voice.

Kristen froze for several moments. She finally turned around slowly, and her face said it all. She knew something.

"It's okay, Mrs. Peters," I said.

"No, it's not okay," Mitch countered.

"I already told you everything I know." Kristen's voice trembled.

"True," Mitch said. "What I want to know is exactly what *aren't* you telling us?"

"Do you want anything to drink?" I asked Kristen as she sat in the interrogation room at the Divinity Police Station.

"Water would be nice." She sat on the edge of her seat, fidgeting with the zipper on her coat.

Mitch had made Ralph stay behind at the inn,

wanting Kristen to be free to say anything and feeling just vulnerable enough to do so.

I handed her a glass of water, and she took a sip as I sat down beside Mitch. We waited for Captain Walker to join us. It felt like the longest ten minutes of my life. Finally, Grady walked in and took a seat on the other side of Mitch, with Kristen across from all of us by herself.

"Hello, Mrs. Peters." Captain Walker smiled. "I hope you're doing well."

"Yes, thank you," she said in a quiet voice. "They've been taking good care of me at the inn."

"Good to hear. That Granny Gert's cookies sure are something, and you won't find a better cook than Great-Grandma Tootsie."

Kristen smiled a genuine smile for the first time and started to relax.

"Detective Stone tells me you have some information about both murders you would like to share with us?"

Kristen tensed all over again.

"Take your time. Whenever you're ready to talk is fine with us. Right, Detective Stone?" I gave Mitch a look that said, *Lighten up if you want to hear anything.* He could be so intimidating at times. He might have left New York City to be a small-town detective, but it was hard to take the homicide grit out of him. And Grady had become too much of a "good cop" to be of much help.

Guess that left me somewhere in the middle.

Mitch gentled his tone a little. "Can you tell us anything about the missing Stillwater woman, Jasmine Jackson?"

"Okay, so this is the thing. I don't know who she is.

And I didn't think anything of Ray having her out to the cabin at the time."

"What changed?" Captain Walker asked.

"Let me start from the beginning. I had an affair with Gunther because I was lonely and he was nice to me. I didn't like what they did, as far as pressuring the local businesses to pay them for their protection, but I stayed out of it. Then I found out Officer Burrows was a crooked cop who turned a blind eye to what was going on, as long as the Rebel Riders gave him a cut of the action. I could no longer ignore what was going on. I was the one who leaked the information to the Stillwater Police Department, and Internal Affairs got involved. I broke things off with Gunther, but it was too late. His ex-girlfriend Renee Jordan had already told Ralph about the affair."

"That's when you ran away with Ray?" I asked.

"Yes. Ray acted so sweet, like he really cared about what happened to me. I thought he was a true friend." Her face turned disgusted. "I should have known better. Ray only cared about one thing. Himself."

"What happened?" Mitch asked.

"Officer Burrows shut their operation down, so Gunther insisted the Rebel Riders start over in a new town. They got a tip that Cole West lived in Divinity, and Gunther became obsessed with revenge. Officer Burrows was angry that the Rebel Riders were moving on without him. He thought they all would lay low until things blew over, then pick up where they left off. But they didn't lay low, and they didn't tell him where they were going. Soon after that, Officer Burrows disappeared. Someone said he took a leave of absence after Internal Affairs didn't have enough evidence on him to stick. I was afraid to come forward before, but I will now. If they ever find him, that is."

"That is all helpful information, Mrs. Peters, but what does this have to do with Ray Simone's death?" Captain Walker asked.

"After I came to Divinity with Ray and the Rebel Riders, Gunther was murdered. The gang took off, and Ray and I started hiding out in the cabin. He wanted to be the new leader of the gang, but none of them respected him like they did Gunther. That made him furious. He was determined to move on and be more successful than they were. He had a chip on his shoulder and something to prove. He started scaring me more than Ralph did, and I began to question my decision to let him help me. Then he started bringing these women to the cabin. All of a sudden, I started seeing men come to the cabin as well. Ray didn't want these women for himself." She looked at Captain Walker. "He started a prostitution ring."

My eyes locked with Mitch's, then I focused back on Kristen. "Did he force you to do anything against your will?"

"No." She swallowed hard. "He tried to."

"That was when you showed up at the inn, isn't it?" Mitch asked, making notes in his notebook.

"Yes. I realized while my husband and I might have issues, I still loved him and I knew he loved me. I thought, when I was drugged and kidnapped, that Ray had found me. But now I'm terrified that Officer Burrows found out about the prostitution ring, and he wanted in on the action. I've heard rumors that he has a few twisted habits he needs money for. If Ray turned him down on cutting him in on the action, he might have killed him. He's crazy enough to do just that. I wouldn't be surprised if he killed Gunther, and then I haven't seen Jasmine since she left the cabin. Who's to say he won't come after me next? I'm terrified."

"We won't let that happen, Mrs. Peters," Captain Walker said.

"Yeah, you know your husband won't let you out of his sight again," I added reassuringly.

"I'll send a detail around the inn periodically." Mitch scanned his notes. "Thank you, Mrs. Peters. You've helped more than you know. I'll fill Detective Torres in, and I'm sure Internal Affairs will want to talk with you if you're up to it."

She nodded and wiped her eyes with the tissues I handed her. "No woman should be forced to do anything against her will."

"As for me, you can bet I'll be following up on a few leads of my own." Mitch stood and gathered his things.

"Where are you going?" I asked.

"To look for some action."

"Need any help with that?" I asked, not liking the sound of that.

"No," he said firmly and frowned at me. "All I want from you is for you to go home." Then he was gone.

"HE REALLY SAID THAT?" ZOE ASKED LATER THAT NIGHT at Smokey Jo's, then took a sip of her wine.

"Yes. 'To look for some action' were his exact words, right after we discovered there was a prostitution ring happening in Divinity." I drained the last of my rocks glass. It was a whiskey kind of night.

"Wait a minute." Jo stopped wiping down the bar. "There's no way you believe Mitch would cheat on you."

"Well, he didn't ask me to go home with him, so he's not looking to get any action from me!" I tapped my empty glass on the bar, and Jo eyed me curiously before refilling my glass. "That can only mean one thing. He's out to see if the prostitution ring is still going on."

"Just how far would he go to solve a case?" Zoe's eyes grew huge.

"Mitch is a very thorough detective." I drained my drink and hopped off the barstool, stumbling a bit. Maybe whiskey wasn't such a good idea after all. "There's only one way to find out."

"Where are you going?" Jo waddled around the bar as fast as she and two babies could go.

"To get a little action of my own."

"Why don't you let your man do his job," Jo pleaded, and placed her hands on my shoulders as if that could stop me.

I reached up to adjust the beanie on my head and spun out of her hold. Little did I know she had signaled for reinforcements. I had only taken five steps before I was whisked off my feet by a sasquatch. "Hey! What are you doing?"

"Saving you from yourself." Cole carried me slung over his massive shoulder the rest of the way through the door.

"Where are we going? I have a date."

"The only date you have is with your pillow, my friend."

"But what about my Grumpy Pants?"

"You let me worry about him. Something tells me he just might need my help even more than you do."

"Why would he let you help him but not me? Because I'm a woman?"

"Yes, frankly." Cole softened his tone before I could protest. "And because you're his fiancé, and he loves you." Cole drove me home in his truck and carried me inside of Vicky before setting me on my feet. "Please, for once, stay put. The last thing Mitch needs is to worry about you. I'll make sure your detective gets home in one piece. And I think I know just where to look."

19

I woke up the next morning and headed to the kitchen for some strong tea. Pouring water in my kettle, I set it on the stove and turned the burner on. Glancing out the window, I sucked in a little breath and my heartbeat sped up. Grumpy Pants was home. His truck was parked by the garage. He must be in his mancave because he hadn't come to bed.

I frowned.

I was in my Tweety Bird pajama bottoms with one of his old NYPD t-shirts and fuzzy slippers. Grabbing a crocheted blanket, I wrapped it around me and picked up my cup of tea, then headed out the door. Even though Mitch was my fiancé, I usually knocked when I entered the garage. I knew that was the one area where he could totally relax, same as my sanctuary was for me. Today, I was feeling too vulnerable. I trusted him completely and knew he wouldn't cheat on me. I just wanted him to treat me as his equal and let me help.

Lifting my hand to knock, I hesitated and reached for the doorknob instead. I pushed the door open, and my heart squeezed. Mitch was sitting on the couch, leaning back, his head to the side sound asleep. I quietly walked over and stood before him. There were notes and files spread all across the coffee table in front of him. I climbed into his lap and spread the afghan over us both, then snuggled into him. He stirred, and his arms instinctively came up to wrap around me and pull me closer.

"You smell good," he mumbled, burying his nose in my butchered hair.

I sniffed then wrinkled my nose. "You don't."

"Sorry," he muttered. "Long night."

I toyed with the string from the hood of his sweatshirt, my cheek pressed against his chest. "Did you find the action you were looking for last night?"

"I did."

My body stilled. "Really? No wonder you're so tired."

"Exhausted." I heard the chuckle in his tone and slapped his chest. He grunted. "Seriously, though. The prostitution ring is definitely still going on."

"Why won't you let me help?"

This time he stilled. "I know you want to help, Tink, but a prostitution ring is no place for a beautiful woman, let alone my fiancé."

"Then don't think of me as your fiancé." I sat up so I could look him in the eye. "Think of me as your partner with an awful haircut and not so beautiful at the moment."

"I'll try."

"Good. Because I would hate for us to take a step back after finally moving forward." I kissed him before he could stick his foot in his mouth, then I climbed off his lap to sit beside him on the couch. "Okay, partner, so tell me what you've got."

He sat up, rubbed his hand through his messy hair, and then studied the papers on the coffee table in front of him. "I searched everywhere I could think of last night, but wasn't having much luck, when Cole miraculously appeared to see if I needed help." Mitch gave me a knowing look.

I examined my nails.

"Pleading the fifth, I see."

I shrugged. "I know my rights."

"Hmmm. Anyway, Cole knows the Rebel Riders and knows all their old haunts. Ray might have split from them, but it stood to reason he might frequent the same spots. Cole took me to some places I'd never even heard of. The prostitution ring is still going on for sure, but I didn't see any sign of Jasmine Jackson. I showed her picture, but no one else has seen her around, either."

"Do you think someone else from the Rebel Riders is running the ring, now that Ray has been murdered?"

"I'm not sure. What I learned pretty quickly is that even if they are, people aren't talking. The gang is feared in more towns than just Stillwater. We're on our own because no one is willing to turn them in."

A knock sounded on the garage door.

I looked at him in question. He stood then grabbed his gun off the end table and slipped it in the back of the waistband of his jeans. It was early morning and our home, but we'd learned in the past that anything can happen at any time. With two murders to solve, the clock ticking and the clues adding up, this was no time to let down our guard. Mitch had turned into Detective Stone once more, and he was through with taking chances.

My detective approached the door from an angle so he wouldn't be in a direct line of fire should anything bad happen. "Who is it?"

"Torres. Open up, man. It's damn cold out here."

Mitch's shoulders relaxed and he opened the door a crack. "Do you know what time it is?" He opened the door wider.

"I know you," Juan said as he entered with two cups of coffee, "and I know you don't sleep until a case is put to bed."

I cleared my throat.

Juan's surprised gaze landed on me. His eyes traveled over my pajamas then Mitch's rumpled hair. "Oh, man—sorry, Sunny. Hope I'm not interrupting anything."

"Nope. No action going on over here. Right Mitch? He's plumb tuckered out from all the action he got last night." I grinned at him, not about to let him off the hook that easily.

He smirked then ignored me. "Why did you say you were here, Torres?"

"I didn't."

"Exactly. Start talking."

Juan handed Mitch a cup of coffee, then turned to me with eyebrows raised in question. I held up my tea. He lifted his cup in salute and took a big drink. "Okay, so Kristen Peters' testimony to Internal Affairs, along with Nancy Culligan's statement that her first blond wig went missing, and confirmation that she is Adam Burrows' sister, led to me getting a search warrant. I went to Burrows' apartment, but he's still out of town in some unknown location. However, the warrant allowed me to search the premises."

"Find anything interesting?" Mitch drained the last of his coffee, drinking it in record time.

"He had lots of pornography on his computer. Flyers for Winterfest in Divinity. We didn't find the wig, but we did find several blond fibers. I sent them to the lab and they match the fibers that were found in the café."

"He must have worn a disguise and trashed the businesses in Divinity, but why?" I set my teacup down and looked through the papers on the coffee table.

"To flush out the Rebel Riders, I'm guessing." Juan finished his coffee as well.

"Burrows was angry over the gang moving on to new territory without him and not cutting him into the profit, which he clearly needs to fund his questionable hobbies. Maybe he killed Gunther and then tried to make it look like the gang was responsible and still in town, pressuring new businesses."

"Yeah," I said, "and maybe when Ray started the prostitution ring, Burrows found out and confronted him. If Ray refused to cut him in, then he could have killed him. And if he's in town, maybe he knows Kristen Peters talked to IA, so he can't go back to Stillwater. Maybe he took over the prostitution ring for money. Clearly someone is running it, based on all the action you saw last night." I fluttered my eyelashes at Mitch.

Detective Torres glanced between the two of us. "Am I missing something?"

"Nothing important." Mitch shook his head at me. "Speaking of missing, I'm beginning to think Jasmine Jackson is in real danger."

"Me too," Torres agreed. "So, what are we going to do about it?"

"I have a plan." I stood up, earning me a confused look from Juan.

"That wouldn't involve looking for some *action*, would it?" Mitch jumped to his feet, his expression grim. He knew me so well.

"Guess you'll have to follow me to find out."

"Over my dead body," Mitch grumbled a couple hours later as we sat in Captain Walker's office.

"Would you please tell him it's the only way," I asked Captain Walker, then sent pleading eyes around the room.

"It does make sense, Mitch," Captain Walker replied.

"Detective Burrows will recognize Mrs. Peters and even you, Detective Stone," Mayor Cromwell stated authoritatively. "Ms. Meadows is our only hope of flushing Burrows out. Or would you prefer to see your best friend go to jail? Because at the moment, Cole West is still the prime suspect. Without his gun, we can't prove it isn't the murder weapon that was used on Gunther Corp. And right now, Adam Burrows is the most logical suspect we have for killing Ray Simone and the only other possible suspect for Gunther Corp's murder. Maybe it's time you start taking your fiancé's abilities a little more seriously."

"This doesn't have anything to do with her abilities." Mitch stood and began to pace around the room.

"Doesn't it?" I asked.

He stopped walking and looked at me. "Sunny, you could be hurt."

"So could you."

"I'm a trained police officer. You're not."

"No, I'm not. However, I would be wearing a wire, and you would be close by."

"She could wear a disguise," Chief Spencer said.

"You too?" Mitch put his hands on his hips and stared at him.

"Listen, Detective, I have to agree with everyone

else." The chief looked me over. "With the proper disguise, Ms. Meadows could pull off being a prostitute."

"Thanks, I think," I said.

Mitch scrubbed a hand over his whiskered face. "I don't like it, but looks like I don't have much of a choice."

"It's settled then." Captain Walker stood. "Sunny, I think it's time you paid a visit to Renee Jordan."

"I'll take her." Mitch grabbed his coat.

"You'll do no such thing." I stood up and grabbed my coat. "I'm a big girl, Detective. I can take care of myself. Besides, I'm not taking a chance of anyone blowing my cover. I'll catch up with you later."

"But—"

"Bye." I waved and walked out of the police station as quickly as possible while I still had backup inside. No matter how worried Mitch was, Mayor Cromwell was right. I was the only solution. Jo and Cole needed me, and I wasn't about to let them down. If Adam Burrows was looking for some action, I'd show him some action.

I would be a prostitute the likes of which this entire county had never seen.

20

That evening, after hours spent in Stillwater, I walked into Smokey Jo's Tavern with purpose in every stiletto step I took. Jo and Cole were behind the bar with Zoe and Sean tending to the tables. Mitch sat on a barstool, drinking a cup of coffee. Tonight was the night we were going to try out my new look.

Who better to try it on first than my fiancé?

The tavern was pretty busy. It was Friday and happy hour had just begun. I made my way past a few tables, earning several looks of appreciation. At least I hoped they were looks of appreciation and not shock.

Renee had outfitted me with a rich, long burgundy wig. The hair was thick, silky straight, and fell to my waist. She'd tinted my eyebrows a shade of red as well, and we used a brown-red mascara and red lipstick to enhance my features. A brown beauty mark on the side of my mouth finished off the look. Hey, if I was playing dress-up, then I had decided to go all out and spice things up a bit. Mitch had liked my Natasha wig so much. I had a feeling my escort look would give him more action than he could ever ask for. Especially with the tight black mini-dress and four-inch heels I had on.

But first we had a killer to catch.

"Oh, I'm sorry," Wally from Wally's World gym said after bumping into me. He smiled. "Where are my manners? Let me buy you a drink to make up for it."

"Okay," I said, feeling confident.

I knew Wally pretty well, but he didn't appear to recognize me. I followed him to the bar, taking the stool right beside Mitch. Here was the real test. He glanced at me, and my heart jumped into my throat. I gave him a little smile. He nodded once, then looked away and continued to talk to Cole.

I released the breath I'd been holding. That was a good sign.

"Hey, Jo, I'll have a..." Wally looked at me.

"Dirty martini, straight up," I answered, making my voice sound deeper and a little more sultry.

Wally looked back at Jo, who cut him off before he could finish.

"Got it." She made the drink in an expert fashion and record time, then set it in front of me. She hesitated for only a second then she smiled. "Here you go...?"

"Ally." I took the drink from her and set it before me. "Thank you...?"

"Joanne West, but you can call me Jo. Everyone does."

I was brought back to the moment I had first met Jo, in what seemed like forever ago at this very bar, when she'd made me a drink and listened to my problems. But today she couldn't know who I was, because I had a job to do. And if I could fool my best friend and my fiancé, then just maybe I stood a chance of fooling a killer.

I turned to Wally. "Thank you, Mr....?"

"Just Wally. And you're welcome. Are you here for the festival? I don't recognize you from Divinity, so I'm assuming you're from out of town."

"I'm from all over, sugar," I said, earning a closer glance from Detective Stone. I kept looking at Wally, but I could feel the curiosity of Mitch's gaze. He was always aware of his surroundings and studying others, especially when working a case.

"How long are you staying?" Wally asked.

"I'm not sure yet." I took a sip of my drink, trying not to wince. It wasn't my drink of choice, but I was playing a character.

"Well, if you need a tour guide, I'm your guy."

"Awww, you're so sweet, hon, but I'm meeting some friends." I looked at the clock behind the bar. "They should be here soon. Thanks anyway."

"Gotcha. Well, maybe I'll see you around?"

"You never know."

Wally left, and I took another sip of liquid courage. I knew the police needed my help, and I was happy to do whatever was necessary for Jo and Cole, but I couldn't deny I was nervous. What if the wire didn't work? What if I lost Mitch? What if I drew out some other pervert and not Adam Burrows? There was so much that could go wrong. I took a deep breath and glanced at the clock again.

"I'm sure your friends will show up sooner or later," Detective Stone leaned over and said to me above the music.

I blinked a few times, taken aback, then quickly returned to character. "Oh, honey, I'm not worried. I just said that to make that man go away. He seemed nice enough, but he really wasn't my type."

"Oh," Mitch responded, sounding surprised. "You seemed so confident with Wally, but then you sounded a little nervous. I was just trying to reassure you. The people are really nice in Divinity. I'm sure you'll have a good time. I'll leave you to your drink." He picked up his coffee and started to turn away.

"Not so fast." I reached out and placed my hand on his forearm. "Now *you* are exactly my type. Care to be my tour guide?"

"Oh, I... no, I couldn't." He patted my hand, then moved it off his arm. "You seem like a nice enough lady, but I'm engaged. In fact, I thought my fiancé was meeting me here." He glanced at his watch. "Must be I heard her wrong. I have someplace I have to be, but enjoy your drink. Jo here is a great bartender. She'll take care of you."

I sighed dramatically. "Pity for me. Oh well, you win some, you lose some. Your fiancé is a lucky girl." I winked.

He frowned. "Right, uh, have a good night, miss." He laid some cash down on the bar. "Thanks for the coffee, Jo. Buy the lady another round on me."

Mitch left, and I bit back a grin. I'd passed the test, and so had my fiancé. It was comforting to know I'd picked a good one.

"What will it be, *Ally*," Jo said, bringing my startled gaze back to hers. "Care to tell me what's going on?"

I should have known I couldn't fool my best friend and a woman as smart as Joanne West for long. She made a living off reading people. But I had fooled my fiancé, and I was going to deal with a man tonight, so I should be fine. "Later, Mrs. West. I have some place I have to be. And I'll take a coffee for the road."

She poured a coffee to go, then handed it to me with a serious expression. "Be careful, miss. Even in small towns, the streets can be scary at night."

"Always." I smiled then headed out the door. Lucky for me I wasn't going to be on any streets, and scary came with the territory for what I had planned.

"WHERE IS MS. MEADOWS, DETECTIVE STONE?" I heard Captain Walker ask from where I stood outside his office.

"Honestly, I thought she would be here already," Mitch answered. "She wasn't at home and she never met me at Smokey Jo's. This is why I didn't think using her as bait was a good idea, but no one wanted to listen to me."

"On the contrary, Detective, I think it's a fabulous idea," I said as I walked up behind him, in the same sultry voice I'd used in the tavern.

He spun around and stared at me, looking confused for a moment. Then his eyes widened as realization dawned. "Sunny?"

"I prefer Ally." I smiled wide, pleased as punch.

"I have to say you look remarkably different," Chief Spencer commented.

"My word, Ms. Meadows, I never would have known that was you." Mayor Cromwell circled around me in awe.

"That's entirely the point, gentlemen. Even my own fiancé didn't recognize me." I kissed Mitch's flushed cheek. "By the way, thank you for not flirting back," I whispered for his ears only, then winked at him.

He just stood there, staring at me, still speechless.

"I do believe this will work," Captain Walker said.

Mitch finally cleared his throat. "I knew there was something off about you, but I couldn't figure out what exactly. I never imagined that was you." He shoved his hands in his pockets. "I still don't like this. What's the plan, then?"

"Detective Torres used his informant's connection and got me a meeting." I brushed non-existent lint off my tight black mini-dress. Mitch was going to like this even less.

"A meeting? With whom? Where?" A muscle in Mitch's cheek pulsed.

"I, um, don't know who I'm meeting, but it's at a cabin in the woods." I rushed through the last part of the sentence not quite making eye contact.

"The same cabin that Ray brought Jasmine Jackson to?" Mitch shot a hard gaze at Chief Spencer. "No disrespect, but *hell* no, this is not happening."

"I'm sorry, Detective, but yes, it is." Chief Spencer looked me over once more in a critical fashion. "Renee Jordan outdid herself. *Ally* is a stranger to Divinity that no one will recognize. She's our only hope to solving these cases."

"Agreed." The mayor looked at the chief. "See that she's well protected. She's important to this department. She's important to our entire town."

"I won't let you down, sir," I said. The mayor had always been one of my biggest fans, and a true believer. It felt good to have him in my corner.

"I know you won't, Ms. Meadows. Just be careful, please. You mean a lot to us all." He patted my arm as he walked by me toward the door. "Keep me informed, Chief."

"Of course, sir." After the mayor left, the chief turned to the captain. "Make sure she's wired correctly and that your men make the right judgement call if she needs you."

"You got it, sir." The chief left and the captain turned to Mitch. "I know I don't have to tell you how to do your job, especially where Sunny is concerned, but please be extra careful. Granny Gert would have my head if she knew what we were up to."

"Roger that," Mitch said, and didn't face me until Grady had left the room.

"I'm going to be okay, Mitch." I touched his back.

He turned around and the worry lines at the corners of his eyes looked deeper. "This is a bad idea, but no one seems to care." He held up his hand to stop me from talking. "I know we don't have any other options, but I don't like this at all. That being said, you know I will do everything in my power to make sure you're safe."

"I know."

"It's you I'm worried about, doing something crazy and impulsive."

I gasped. "Me? When do I ever do anything like that?"

He grunted. "Only every other day."

"Well, I won't tonight. I promise."

He went over and locked the door to his office, then closed the blinds on the window. "Pull down your dress."

"I know you like Ally even better than Natasha, but can't you wait until later?" I giggled, reaching for the neckline of my dress.

He ignored me and held up the wire.

"Oh." My grin faded, and I could feel the heat flood my face as I complied then held out my arms to my sides. "Wire away."

Mitch's gaze widened as he took in the racy lingerie I wore. "Why?" He gaped at me. "I certainly hope no one is going to see these."

"Of course not. I wore them to put myself in character and help me stay in character and... well... for *you* later."

"Good answer." His lips tipped up in a slight grin for the first time in days. Then he proceeded to strategically place the wire around my stomach and between my breasts. He helped me pull my dress back up when he was done, albeit way more slowly than was probably necessary.

"Thank you," I said, just inches from his mouth.

He kissed me softly in response then pulled me in for a long hug. "Please be careful, Tink. Be alert and talk to me, okay?"

"I will. I promise. Everything will be okay as long as we stick to the plan."

21

"Can you hear me?" I said while walking along a plowed path in my four-inch high-heeled boots which zipped up above my knees. I tightened the faux fur wrap around my black mini-dress. The forecast called for more snow, so I'd made a last-minute change in footwear, not that these boots offered any kind of traction, but they did keep my legs warmer.

The instructions I received were to get dropped off at the campgrounds office, and then make my way alone to cabin number ten. Detective Stone and Detective Fuller, as well as a few other officers, were strategically placed throughout the woods, but far enough away not to be seen. I knew the men were close by, but I still felt eerily alone and creeped out. I had to stay focused and remember why I was doing this. I would do anything for Jo and Cole.

"Roger that," Mitch responded. "I hear you, but Tink, try to maintain radio silence unless absolutely necessary."

"Copy that." I used the flashlight on my phone to see the path in front of me. The woods were so dark this far back, and my toes were frozen. At least we hadn't had any recent snowfall, so the snowpack was solid beneath my feet, crunching softly beneath my boots. It felt like forever before I reached the cabin. Oh, Lord, deja vu set in.

This was the same cabin where Ray had taken Jasmine Jackson.

I glanced one last time at the woods around me, but didn't see anything through the ominous darkness. I had been totally on board with this idea, but now that I was here, my nerves were getting the best of me. I had to keep reminding myself that Mitch was nearby and just a scream away.

I knocked on the door and waited, trying not to shiver. I had to stay in character and bury my nerves. My heartbeat tripped into overdrive as I heard footsteps on the other side. The door opened, and I blinked.

Wayne Emerson stood before me.

His broken nose from when Ray had punched him had started to heal, his black eyes nearly normal now. I hadn't really seen him since then because he'd shut down his booth after most of his woodwork pieces had been destroyed. Ray had said Wayne destroyed them, but Kristen had confided that Ray was the one who had done it. I felt bad for Wayne over having such a bad first experience at Winterfest, and had thought he probably wouldn't return next year.

The more I thought about it, I wasn't really surprised to see him here. Kristen did say he had made some lewd comments toward her when he'd hit on her. It made sense he would be into something like prostitution. Maybe he had a hard time getting a woman interested in him any other way. I waited a beat to see if he recognized me, but he didn't seem to.

All I saw in his eyes was passion as he looked me over. I swallowed hard and tried to keep calm.

"Please, come in." He stepped back and held the door open.

I walked inside and a strong feeling of doom settled over me. I sucked in a breath. I wasn't sure if I was picking up negative vibes from when Jasmine was here with Ray. I tried to take in every aspect of the cabin, looking for clues to her whereabouts. Anything that might help that I could relay to Mitch.

"Are you okay?" Wayne closed the door behind me. I could hear him moving around the cabin.

"I'm fine." I took a moment to compose myself before I turned around to face him. "I just stubbed my toe."

"Don't be nervous." He called my bluff as he took a step toward me, and it was all I could do not to step back.

"I'll admit, I'm a little nervous. I'm fairly new to the scene." I figured stick as close to the truth as possible.

"I'll take care of you." He walked past me to a sideboard against the far wall. He poured whiskey into two glasses then returned to me and handed me one. "This will help you to relax. I don't bite."

I took the glass from him and stared down at the ice ball with rich amber liquid swirling around it. He lifted his glass and took a healthy swallow, so I did the same. The liquid burned a path down my throat and warmed my belly.

"This place is cozy." I took in the rustic cabin, my eyes briefly landing on the king-sized bed, then quickly moving on. I didn't see any signs that Jasmine had been here or any clues to where she might be now.

He shrugged. "It's okay, but not what I paid for."

"Oh, yeah? Paid who?"

"To be honest, I'm not really sure." He wiped his blond mustache with a napkin and set his drink down. "Everything is anonymous."

"Really?" I walked around the cabin, picking up various items, trying to get a read on anything as I stalled. "I heard some guy named Adam had taken over after Ray."

"Look, darlin', I don't know his name. I just know Divinity has been a huge disappointment for me." Wayne sounded irritated, and if what Kristen and Ray had said was true, I didn't want to set the guy off. I would have to choose my words more carefully in trying to get information out of him.

"Whoever took over for Ray offered me a discount because of all I've been through, but I don't take charity." He trailed his fingertips down my arm. "I paid double for an extra special experience."

"Oh, I see." I let out a nervous laugh and tried to step out of his reach without being obvious. "Then, um, how do I get my cut?"

His forehead wrinkled. "You really are new to this."

"Okay, you got me. This is my first time, You're my first. My friend Jasmine told me about this opportunity and set it up for me, but I haven't seen her in a while. Do you know her? Jasmine Jackson?"

"The name doesn't ring a bell, but here's how this all works. I pay the man in charge of the operation—at least I'm assuming it's a man, but you never know nowadays—and then you get your cut through an app."

"Ah, yes, I remember setting that up." I hadn't, but I was just going with the flow and winging it.

"All I know is I paid top dollar. This small cabin in

the woods is *not* what I had in mind." He looked at his watch, and then studied me as if he were waiting for something. "Let's go someplace else. I intend to get my money's worth."

My eyes widened. "Someplace else?" I dropped my chin a little and spoke louder. "You're taking me someplace else?" My eyes felt heavy suddenly, my limbs weak, like it took so much energy to move them even a little bit.

"Yes, *Sunny*, I am."

That was the last thing I heard. I watched the passion leave his eyes replaced by a hard burning anger that filled my insides with ice. The feeling of doom intensified until I felt like I was suffocating as I collapsed on the floor.

———————

MY EYES FELT SEALED SHUT AND GRITTY. COLD SEEPED through my every cell clear to my bones. My muscles ached and felt heavy. The smell of musty, stale air penetrated my senses. I pried my eyelids open to the first rays of daylight filtering through the dirty windows. This cabin was far worse than the other cabin. It had a couple bunkbeds, old ratty furniture, and ancient appliances. How was this better than the last cabin? Confusion clouded my senses.

I sat up then quickly slapped a hand over my chest. My dress was shoved down to my waist, my bra still in place, thank goodness. I bit my lip. The wire was gone. My hand shot to my head. So was my wig. I searched the cabin, but I was alone. There was no heat or fire in the woodstove. No wonder I was freezing. I pulled my dress back up then stood up from the lumpy bare mattress. My boots were still on, but my warm wrap was gone.

My head spun. Obviously, Wayne Emerson had drugged my glass of whiskey. When had he discovered who I was? I remembered him calling me Sunny before I blacked out. I walked over to the kitchen sink and looked out the window. There was a snowmobile parked there. We were somewhere deep in the woods in what I was guessing was an old hunting cabin. My stomach turned sour. It was the next morning.

Mitch must be frantic.

I had no way of knowing where we were or how to reach him. He had to know something was off because he heard the end of our conversation, but I had no idea if he was able to follow us. Probably not, because he wouldn't have waited until morning to rescue me. Stone cold fear filled my being. If I got out of this in one piece, I was never going to question his judgement again. His gut had told him for me not to go, and he had been right. Sometimes I could be so stubborn.

The door suddenly opened, and I whirled around with hope.

Wayne looked angry and disappointed, and my shoulders wilted. My hope evaporated and all I felt was defeated. He carried wood inside and shut the door behind him. Without saying a word, he stacked the wood in the stove and lit it, then closed the door. I could feel the heat already and finally stopped shivering. He took a moment to warm his hands before turning around to face me, then I started shivering for a different reason.

Rage. A deep burning rage simmered in his blue eyes.

"I thought you were my friend, Ms. Meadows."

"I am," I rushed to say. "I didn't know you would be my client."

"You know what I've been through. Why would you wear a wire and try to set me up? Do you want to see me arrested? Prostitution's illegal you know. I can't go to jail. It would ruin me."

"I'm not trying to ruin you. I swear. I thought you were someone else. You're not the one we're looking for. I won't tell anyone that you were my client. Let me go, and I'll say my client was a stranger and he ran away."

"It's too late. You saw my face," he looked me in the eyes, "and I don't trust you. Your fiancé is a cop."

"I didn't say your name, and I won't. No one will know who you are." I actually meant that. I would say or do anything at this moment if it meant gaining my freedom.

He seemed to hesitate for a moment, then he looked at me with pity. It was scary how quickly he switched between anger and pity. Like someone had flipped a switch. "I like you, Sunny, I do, but I can't take the risk."

"I'm no risk at all." I took a step backwards. "I'll go away. Disappear. You'll never see me again."

"I guess you really are psychic, because that is exactly what is going to happen." He pulled out a 9-millimeter handgun and started to walk toward me.

I had to do something. I couldn't just give up. Suddenly having children or not, I knew I couldn't live without my grumpy pants detective. Adrenaline roared through me. I faked left, surged right, then darted around Wayne. He dropped his gun over my unexpected movements and reached for me. The moment he touched my skin; I froze. My eyes turned to tunnel vision, and I was in Ray Simone's body. I felt the anger take over me, but I felt the anger coming from Wayne even stronger.

Pure uncontrollable rage.

The next thing I knew his hands were on my neck. Ray's neck. But I felt everything Ray had felt. I couldn't breathe. I clawed at his hands to no avail. I felt helpless. I was in shock, then fear, then pain, then numbness settled in. Fear shook me followed by the realization I was going to die and there wasn't a damn thing I could do about it.

A force shoved me away.

Blinking my eyes rapidly, I wiped away tears. I grabbed my throat, but it was fine. I hadn't been strangled. Ray Simone had. And the man before me had done it. Wayne Emerson had killed Ray Simone.

I focused on Wayne and noticed the scratches I had clawed on his face and his blond mustache was crooked. *Crooked*? My lips parted as I lifted my gaze to his. Realization dawned in Wayne's eyes, and he reached up to pull off his blond wig. He ran a hand through his matted red hair and pulled his mustache the rest of the way off.

My heart jumped into my throat then plummeted to my toes.

"You see why I can't let you go, Sunny? Because I *am* the man you're looking for after all."

Wayne Emerson didn't kill Ray Simone. Adam Burrows did. And the way things were looking, I was next.

22

"**D**etective Burrows, you don't have to do this," I pleaded, trying to stall until I could figure out what to do. How had I missed the signs? I'd always thought his hair and mustache looked off somehow, but never imagined he was wearing a wig. I'd believed Wayne when he'd said he paid an app and didn't know who the man in charge was.

He'd been in charge all along.

He picked up his gun and stared at it. "*Detective*?" He laughed harshly. "That's over." His harsh grin turned into a frown. "All I ever wanted to be was a cop. I was a damn good one too, but being a police officer doesn't pay much. Things were better when I became a detective," his eyes met mine, "but a man has needs. Needs which are expensive." His gaze traveled over me as if he were contemplating just how soon he had to kill me. We were alone in the middle of the woods, after all. Who would know?

My skin crawled.

"As a man of the law, you know there are always deals that can be made." I tried to think of anything to stall him. The man had clearly lost his marbles. "I'm sure if you cooperate, they'll—"

"I killed people, Ms. Meadows. If I go to prison, I'll never leave. As a police officer, I'll be killed long before dying of old age." His lips flattened into a hard line. "I can't go to prison. That means I can't have any witnesses. I didn't want to kill Jasmine, but she recognized me from Stillwater."

My heart sank over that news.

"Poor girl's neck was much easier to squeeze than Ray's. I may have a lot of flaws, but I'm not a born killer. I especially didn't like killing a woman, but I couldn't risk her turning me in." Anger flooded his face. "Killing Ray was a pleasure. He thought he was such a big shot moving on without me. All I wanted was a cut of the action like before. It's his fault I had to kill him."

"I don't blame you for killing Ray. He double-crossed you when you had a deal." I slowly took a step back toward the kitchen sink. If I could just reach the knife on the counter, I might stand a fighting chance.

"I didn't plan it. The killing was an accident."

My boot heel scraped on the floor.

His head snapped in my direction. "Stop moving." He waved his gun about, talking with his hands just like Raoulle had. Only this time it wasn't just hair I would lose. "I know what you're doing," he went on. "You're trying to distract me. It won't work."

"I'm not. I'm just nervous and not used to wearing high heels. And, well, I really don't want to die."

He seemed to think about that, but then lifted his hands. "I'm sorry. I don't want to kill you, but I don't have a choice."

"Everyone has a choice. I told you I won't tell anyone. No one knows Wayne Emerson is you." I took a step toward him. "Let me do a reading for you. You don't have to live in the past. I have a feeling your future will be much brighter."

"Murder takes away a person's choices. Once someone crosses the line that far, there's no going back." His gaze met mine and locked. "You're marrying a detective. I'm not stupid, Sunny. If your detective is any good, which I happen to know he is, then he will get the information out of you." He waved his gun toward the door of the cabin. "I'm tired of our conversation. Move."

"It's freezing out there." I rubbed my numb arms, my gaze scanning the cabin. "Can I grab my wrap?"

"You won't be cold for long." He shoved me toward the door.

I stumbled several steps until I cleared the doorway. My dress was long-sleeved, and he'd left my boots on, thank goodness. Although they were more of a spring boot, they were better than bare feet.

"You might not have intended to murder anyone, but you're intentionally being heartless by making me suffer."

"I lost your coat on the snowmobile ride here." He lifted one shoulder. "Sorry. I couldn't exactly go back for it with half the police department after me."

"What about your coat?" I asked, looking around for an escape route.

"Like I said, you won't need it for long. I will."

"Where are we going?" I asked.

"Just keep walking."

The sun was shining on the pristine white snow, but all I could think about was how messy it would soon be if he shot me. I was shivering uncontrollably now. We walked probably fifty feet, when we came to a fresh grave. I swallowed hard, my stomach twisting into knots.

That had to be Jasmine's.

"I made the mistake of dumping Ray in the river. I thought with the water being frozen, the current beneath the ice would take him far enough away from Divinity, and no one would discover his body until the spring. I didn't count on the ice fishing competition and him being the catch of the day."

That was an understatement, I thought, but was too afraid to say anything.

"I won't make that mistake again." He stopped walking behind me, the woods eerily quiet. I could hear my heart beat in my ears, and the sound of his heavy breathing behind me. "Pick up the shovel and start digging."

I turned around slowly to look at him with my hands in the air. "You're kidding, right? The ground is frozen, and I'm not nearly strong enough to dig."

"Try anyway."

I picked up the shovel and tried to shove it into the ground to no avail. Even if I'd wanted to, there was no way that would happen. Looking at him, I shrugged. "See? Looks like you won't be able to kill me after all."

"Nice try. It doesn't really matter, I guess." He raised his gun, pointed it straight at my head and cocked it. "Nobody comes out here in the winter, and the wildlife will dispose of your remains come spring."

I closed my eyes tight. This was it. I was going to die before ever getting to marry the love of my life. I thought of my parents and of the children I'd never have. I thought of Jo and the babies I would never get to meet. I thought of never getting to grow old and never having another argument with my grumpy pants. And I thought of Morty. How would I ever live without seeing my kindred spirit again?

A hissing noise came from the side, and I could

have cried. I whipped my eyes open to see Morty with hackles raised, fangs showing and eyes glowing.

"What the hell...?" Adam turned his gun on Morty, and my heart bottomed out.

"No!" I shouted and dove to the side without giving it a second thought. All that ran through my mind was I couldn't lose either of the most important guys in my life, as I felt the searing heat of a bullet penetrate my flesh... then the world went black.

"Tink, wake up. You have to be okay. I can't live without you. Whatever it takes, I'll do it." I felt big warm hands on my face. "Please, baby, don't leave me." Mitch's voice came to me as if through a dream.

Was I dead? Was my detective with me?

My heart started pounding over that thought. Not so much over the thought of my own death, but I couldn't bear for anything bad to happen to my soul-mate or my sidekick. Speaking of sidekicks...

Morty!

I surged up, then cried out in pain and dropped back down. All my senses came flooding back at once on a rush of feelings. Cold, numb toes and fingers ached something fierce, and pinpricks raced all along my arms and legs as my body felt the blood rush back in. Then the horrible throbbing pain in my shoulder brought back the memory of what had happened.

I'd been shot by Adam Burrows.

"Sunny, talk to me," Mitch said louder.

I definitely wasn't dead. "You don't have to yell." I pried my eyes open, fear nearly rendering me speech-less, but I had to know. "Where's Morty?" I finally managed to get out.

227

"There's my sassy girl." Mitch's strong rugged features wilted with relief. "Thank God you're okay."

"Morty? Was he hurt?"

"Not at all. I mean, we're talking about Morty here. I'm the one who's a mess." He scrubbed a hand over his face, and I had to admit he looked terrible. "I've been terrified and trying to find you all night, Sunny. Once your wire cut out, we had no way of tracking you. I had just about given up hope, which I have to say was the worst experience of my life. When Morty showed up out of nowhere with blood on his paws, I thought maybe he was hurt at first. Sure, we're still not on the best of terms, but I wanted to help. That darn cat wouldn't let me touch him. When he kept fussing and not hissing at me, I immediately knew he had been with you. He was pretty persistent in wanting me to follow him, so I did. He led us here."

"Us?"

Mitch moved aside so I could see every possible 911 department had arrived.

"Where is he?" I needed to see that he was okay for myself.

"Once he led us here, he disappeared as usual."

"But you said his paws were bloody."

"I'm guessing he's fine. The blood isn't his."

"Is it mine?" I asked, afraid of what I might find. I lifted my fingers up to feel a big bandage on my shoulder.

"No, it's not your blood. You were shot, but the bullet went clean through your shoulder. You were lucky. The guy who shot you... not so much." Again, he moved aside and helped me to sit up.

My eyes widened as I took in the sight of Adam Burrows buried neck deep in the hole he wanted me to dig. The ground had been frozen solid. Who had dug the hole? Adam's face was clawed and bloody, his eyes looking as if he were in shock as the police tried to dig him back out.

"But how...?"

"I'm guess Morty gave him a taste of his own medicine. He hurt him, buried him, but left him alive so he could suffer a worse fate by going to jail."

I closed my eyes for a moment, loving my cat more than ever. When I opened my teary eyes again, I said, "Adam killed Ray and Jasmine."

"I know. We found her grave and his gun. A 9-millimeter. I'm betting he killed Gunther as well." Mitch cupped my face and stroked a thumb over my cheekbone. "As much as I hate to admit this, we wouldn't have caught him if it wasn't for you."

"As much as I hate to admit this, that was the scariest thing I've ever done. I should have listened to you."

"Wait, can you repeat that?"

"No." I laughed softly, then winced at the pain. "Cole and Jo will be so relieved. We should go tell them. Can we go home now?"

"No way. *We* aren't doing anything. You're going straight to the hospital. And this time I don't want any arguments."

"Okay."

"Okay?" He stared at me with skepticism written all over his handsome face. "What's the catch?"

"No catch." I took his hand in mine and held on tight. "When you have your life flash before your eyes, it tends to set your priorities straight."

His face looked so serious. "My thoughts exactly."

"What does that mean?"

"It means I love you."

"I love you too, but—"

"We'll talk later." He wrapped me up in a blanket and carried me to an ambulance. "Right now, I need to know you're okay for real."

For once, I didn't argue because I knew exactly how he felt. I'd had a moment of clarity. I didn't know for certain what the future held in store for us, but I *did* know I wanted that future to involve a wedding with me becoming the wife of one Detective Grumpy Pants.

23

"Here you go, darling, have some more tea." My mother poured more hot water into my cup, waiting on me hand and foot and insisting I stay at the inn while I recovered. Morty had been waiting for me when I arrived home from the hospital and hadn't left my side since. He didn't have a scratch on him, but I had to admit I didn't want him out of my sight either.

"Mother, I was shot in the shoulder. I can still fend for myself." As much as I appreciated all the attention, I felt suffocated. And I'd only been here for a few hours. Her face fell for a moment before she covered up her feelings like she always did. "I'm sorry, Mom. I really am grateful for everything." I took a sip of my tea and smiled wide. "Yummy."

She looked pleased with herself. It had been a battle all day between her and the Tasty Trio over who could take care of me and Morty the best. Morty squirmed, sporting a new bowtie, compliments of Granny Gert. And his fur was all fluffy from the bath Great-Grandma Tootsie had given him. I sniffed and wrinkled my nose over the cologne Auntie Fiona had sprayed on him. He stared into my eyes, and I sighed, thinking, *I know, buddy. I can't wait to go home, either.*

The doorbell rang. I jumped up, and Morty bolted off my lap. "Got it," I hollered, but not quite quick enough.

"You'll do no such thing of the sort." My father cut me off and pointed a finger at the couch, sporting a look I hadn't seen since I was ten.

My shoulders drooped and I sat back down.

"You, too, mister." He motioned for Morty to join me on the couch, and my cat actually listened. I felt like I was living in an alternate universe.

Harry answered the door and returned a moment later with my fiancé. I gave Mitch a look that said, *Help!* His lips twitched a little, but that was it. I was beginning to think he'd orchestrated the whole thing for me to stay put and out of trouble, and for Morty to babysit me. There was no need. We had our killer. Case closed. Hence, there was *no* reason I had to stay here.

I narrowed my eyes at him.

He ignored me and sat down in the chair by the couch, his face turning serious as he pinched the bridge of his nose.

I knew that look and nothing good ever came from it. "What's wrong?" I asked, dread filling me.

He looked exhausted, and I was pretty sure he hadn't slept in the past twenty-four hours. "Turns out Adam Burrows' gun is not the one that killed Gunther."

My heart sank. "Really? I was so certain."

"I was hopeful as well, but at least he's still in jail for killing Ray and Jasmine. He won't be able to hurt you anymore."

"Then why the long face?"

"I've been working nonstop, especially when I thought this case was finally wrapped up. What I discovered after ruling out Adam is that our other leads aren't panning out either." He pulled out his notebook and flipped through it. "Gretta came forward when she realized she was working in her grocery store and saw Ralph at the time of Gunther's murder. He wasn't even at the motorcycle expo center."

"That's good for Ralph and Kristen at least."

"True." He looked through more of his notes. "Then there's Renee."

"What about her?"

"Raoulle informed me she was trading secrets with him in his salon at the time of Gunther's murder, so she now has an alibi as well." Mitch closed his notebook and rubbed the back of his neck as he closed his eyes for a moment.

"I didn't think Renee was guilty of murdering Gunther. She might have been hurt and angry, but she still loved him. I'm happy for her. She's not a bad person. In fact, she's been very helpful to me."

"I agree, Tink," he opened his eyes and looked at me with genuine concern, "but I'm *not* happy."

"Why?"

"Cole's gun is still missing, and we're out of suspects."

"Oh..." I let out a big breath.

"Yeah." He leaned his head back and Morty actually jumped on his lap. He didn't even flinch like he would have in the old days. He just absently stroked Morty's back, and Morty purred.

My heart completely melted, and I finally felt complete. Until I remembered what this news would do to my best friend. "When are you going to tell Cole?"

"Not today," Zack said with Cathy in the foyer as they put their coats on.

I hadn't even heard them arrive.

"Sorry to eavesdrop," Cathy said. "I came to pick Zack up. He's helping out at West Construction today."

"The last thing Cole needs is to lose hope," Zack said with a firm tone, and Cathy nodded in agreement. "He's innocent. We all know that. The truth always comes out eventually. Until then, I intend to keep his spirits up as one of his best friends."

"Roger that." Mitch rubbed his hands together, and Morty jumped off his lap. "I'm not giving up. There has to be something we're missing. You can bet I won't stop until I find it." He stood. "I've got work to do. Will you be okay here?" he asked me.

"No, but I will be okay at Smokey Jo's." I stood and walked past him. Only after donning my coat did I respond. "Tonight is the chili cookoff. As one of Jo's best friends, I intend to support her as well." I looked around, but Morty had already disappeared.

"Fair enough." Mitch joined us at the door. "Looks like we all have a job to do, but we'd better get out of here before the posse stops us."

He didn't have to tell me twice.

"WOW, THAT TASTES GREAT, JO." I WIPED MY MOUTH with a napkin.

"You think so?" She stood behind the bar, stressing over her presentation, wanting everything to be perfect. The judges would make the rounds among all the restaurants participating and sample everyone's chili, then reconvene at the judge's stand on Main Street, with a community bonfire to follow.

"I think this is the year you're going to beat Nikko." He ran the Italian restaurant and served a top-secret chili recipe his mama had given him, which was the winner every year. Maybe this was the year for a change. Jo had outdone herself this year. Maybe it was because she was in nesting mode at the end of her pregnancy. Whatever the reason, she had created magic this time around.

"She's a winner," Cole said, as he walked through the front door with Cathy and Zack. Miles, Sean and Zoe were already here while Mitch was still looking for that missing piece of the puzzle.

"I've been hearing great buzz from the tables." Zoe approached the bar and set empty bowls on the counter for Sean to take to the back. Filling her tray with new bowls, she returned to the waiting tables.

"I wish I could help," I said, but I only had one good arm.

"No way. Your fiancé will kill me if I let you lift a finger," Jo said.

"I can help." Miles jumped up, and Jo gladly handed him an apron.

Cathy and Zack sat at the bar with me, while Cole went in the back to help Sean keep the chili coming.

"How did today go at the construction office?" I asked. "Did he seem okay?" I motioned my head toward the swinging door where Cole had just disappeared, not wanting to say his name out loud or bring any attention to our conversation. Especially from Jo. She was busy manning the bar and didn't need any distractions or any more to worry about.

Cathy shrugged. "He's okay. He puts on a brave

face when he's with Jo, but I can see the strain on him
at work."

"He's about the best person I know." Zack shook
his head. "I've known him forever. Sure, he's made
mistakes in the past. We all have. He doesn't deserve to
have the rest of his life ruined."

"Don't worry. Justice will prevail. It always does,"
Miles said from behind us as he rounded the bar and
refilled his tray with more bowls of chili. "You guys
might want to lower your voices, though." He jerked
his head to the side toward Jo who was headed in our
direction. "She's a little fragile these days."

Now there was a sentence I never expected to hear
anyone utter.

"Thanks so much for your help, Miles." Jo
squeezed his arm. "Things are going much more
smoothly now." Worry lines I hadn't noticed before
creased the corners of her eyes and her cheeks looked
a little drawn.

"My pleasure," Miles said. "And I'm with Sunny. I
think this chili is the winner." He winked.

"From your lips to the judges' ears." She went back
to the other end of the bar to fix more presentations.

"It really is delicious." Cathy ate the last spoonful
from her bowl.

"It is good, but a little spicy for my tastes." Zack
coughed. He took a drink of water, then coughed
again.

"You do look a little flushed." Cathy studied his
face. "Are you allergic to anything? Your face looks a
little puffy."

"Not that I know of, but something is definitely
bothering my throat." He went into a full-blown
coughing fit. He stood and stumbled a bit, then his

eyes rolled back in his head and he collapsed on the floor.

"Zack!" Cathy shrieked, slapping her hands over her mouth and looking like she was in shock.

I tried to touch Cathy's arm to reassure her, but she flinched and jumped away. She just kept shaking her head no, over and over, with tears streaming down her face.

Miles looked at her, startled, then dropped to his knees. "Zack, buddy, speak to me." He felt for a pulse.

"Oh, no," Jo grabbed her belly, "this can't be happening again."

"Tell me he's not dead, man." Cole gripped his apron in his huge hands. He and Sean had rushed from the back after the noise from the crowd had increased.

"He has a pulse, but it's weak. Better call 911. The rest of you, stand back." Miles stood guard over Zack, still trying to revive him until the ambulance showed up.

Suddenly, winning the chili cookoff was the last thing on anyone's mind.

24

"What's up?" Mitch asked Cole at West Construction the next morning. He'd been working all night, trying to solve this latest mystery.

"You sounded urgent when you called us." I'd followed Mitch, not about to miss whatever Cole had to say. Since Mitch wanted to keep an eye on me, he'd agreed. Neither of us had been able to sleep after Zack had ended up in the hospital. Jo had been so upset, her doctor had sent her home and ordered her to bed rest. Miles and Cathy had gone to the hospital while Zoe and Sean had closed the Tavern. The chili cookoff had been cancelled with no winner, sending Mayor Cromwell into fits.

"This is what's up." Cole reached into his drawer and pulled out his 9-millimeter hand gun and set it on his desk.

"Wait, I don't get it," I said. "If someone was trying to set you up, then why would they return the murder weapon?"

"Because it's not the murder weapon," Cole said, inspecting the gun. "It hasn't been fired in years. Not by me or anyone else."

"I'll take it to the station and have it tested, but this is great news, Cole." Mitch bagged the gun. "It will clear your name."

"What about the real murderer?" Cole asked. "I heard that Burrows' gun wasn't used to kill Gunther."

"Someone who owns a 9-millimeter handgun killed Gunther, then stole your gun and tried to frame you."

"The question is who and why?" I asked.

"That's what I intend to find out."

"Another thing," Cole said. "Cathy hasn't shown up yet today, and she's always here before me."

"Maybe she's sick like Zack. I thought he had an allergic reaction, but maybe it's food poisoning. Although, no one else got sick from Jo's chili," I said.

"It's neither of those. I didn't have a chance to tell you yet," Mitch looked at me, "but I talked to the doctor at the hospital. Zack was poisoned."

"Poisoned?" Cole's eyebrows shot sky high.

"The tavern was packed with people who live here as well as out of towners. Anyone could have slipped something into his bowl. But why Zack?"

"I have no clue, but I don't have a good feeling about Cathy not showing up." A muscle in Cole's cheek tightened. "She didn't call in sick, and I called the hospital just before you got here. Miles said she left after visiting hours like he did, but she hasn't shown up there this morning yet."

"Do you think the murderer is targeting people close to you?" Mitch asked.

"It sure looks that way." Cole made a fist.

"Let's rule out all the places Cathy could be before you go off half-cocked and wind up in trouble again. Got it?" Mitch gave Cole a warning look.

Cole nodded and relaxed his fist.

"First things first. Let's check in with everyone," I said. "Something tells me this nightmare isn't over with yet."

―――――――

"THIS IS INSANE," JO SAID. SHE SAT AT A TABLE IN Smokey Jo's. "Can't anything good ever happen? We finally clear Cole's name, yet we're still in danger."

"It will all be okay." Zoe took her hand. "You need to go back home and rest, Jo. You heard what the doctor said."

"I feel helpless not doing anything."

"You are doing something. You're taking care of your babies," I said.

"I'm not going anywhere," Sean said. "I promise I won't let anything happen to any of you or the babies."

"I just can't believe Zack was poisoned," Miles said, worry lines creasing his brow. "The only good thing is by staying in the hospital he can finally detox. He's been addicted to pain killers for years because of his war injuries."

"That poor guy," I said. "And now Cathy's missing? Who's next?"

"We're not going to sit back and find out," Cole said.

"Count me in." Miles stood. "What do you have planned?"

"Nothing without me." Detective Stone walked in at that moment. He'd been gone since leaving the construction office with Cole's gun. "Sean, you stay with the ladies and man the bar. Zoe, you look after Jo. Cole and Miles, you're coming with me."

"And me." I jumped up, ready for the mission at hand.

"Not a chance, Tink."

"From what we've just discovered, this murder investigation is still ongoing. Captain Walker said divide and conquer. Since you don't want me investigating on my own, then you have no choice but to let me join you."

Mitch rubbed his temples and shrugged. "In some odd way, that made sense. Or I've simply lost my mind. Either way, I don't have time to think on it. The first forty-eight hours someone's missing is critical in getting them back. Let's move out."

I grabbed my coat and led the way out the door before Grumpy Pants could change his mind.

WE'D SEARCHED THE TOWN, MADE CALLS FOR ANY place she might have gone to out of town, and then turned to the woods. After looking for hours, Cole stopped abruptly and bent down to inspect the ground.

"Wait. These are footprints." Cole bent closer to the ground. "It snowed a little last night, so the tracks are fresh. Looks like two sets of prints with one set being bigger than the others."

Miles joined him. "This brings back memories of when you, Zack, and I used to track deer." He smiled a little along with Cole, then they both grew serious as he inspected the ground as well. "You're right." He followed the tracks with his gaze and then pointed off in the distance. "Looks like they lead to that cabin over there."

Mitch stepped in front of us all. "Stay close." He motioned for me to get behind him. I gladly complied, more than happy for once to let him take the lead.

Being in charge was overrated, I decided, as I rubbed my wounded shoulder.

"There's a light on," I said as we drew close. I frowned, the first seed of doubt taking root. "The killer could still be in there."

We crept forward slowly so as not to alert the killer if he was in the cabin still. Mitch scanned the area and then peeked in the window. He motioned for us to stay to the side out of danger in case the killer had a gun.

"Police, open up."

Nothing.

"Police, open up," Mitch repeated.

Still nothing.

He drew his weapon and carefully reached for the door handle. It wasn't locked. He turned the nob and swung the door open, then did a sweep of the cabin before returning to the door. "All clear. Cathy's here alone." He slid his gun back in its holster and stood aside so we could enter.

I rushed over to Cathy and started to untie her hands. Her eyes were huge, and she shook her head no. As soon as I touched her, I froze. My eyes narrowed into tunnel vision like they always did when I picked up a reading, the present fading away.

Zack broke into Cole and Jo's house, and Cathy was right behind him.

"You don't have to do this, Zack," Cathy said.

"I don't have a choice. I need the drugs," Zack replied. "The pain is unbearable without them."

"There has to be another way," she pleaded, sounding desperate.

"There's not. That's why I didn't want to get close to you. I tried to think of anything else I could do, but I'm in too deep."

"Well, it's too late. You're stuck with me. I'm not letting you go down alone." She opened the safe and took out Cole's gun. "I'll take care of hiding it. You do the rest."

I jerked my hands away and gasped, blinking back to my normal vision. My whole body shook. I'd felt his pain and finally understood what Morty had been trying to tell me with his limping and stumbling about as if he were on drugs. He'd been pointing me toward Zack all along, but I'd missed his cues. My gaze settled on Cathy. Tears welled in her eyes, her hands still tied and mouth still duct-taped. I couldn't believe either one of them would betray Cole this way.

"Cathy stole your gun and hid it," I said, turning to face Cole. This was going to tear him apart. "I saw it all." I closed my eyes for a moment and whispered Morty's name. I wasn't sure what the extent of my abilities were, I just knew we were connected. He'd come every time before when I was in danger or hurt. I was hoping he would feel me and know I needed him more than ever.

"What?" Miles gaped at me as my words registered, then he turned accusing eyes on Cathy.

"Cathy? How? *Why*?" Cole asked, looking stunned and then devastated. "I don't understand."

"She didn't work alone," I clarified, knowing this next part was going to hurt. "Zack was with her. He was in bad shape. He killed Gunther for drug money."

"That's crazy," Miles shook his head.

"Wait a minute. Then why return the gun?" Mitch asked, always the voice of reason when emotions were running high. "This doesn't make sense. And Zack didn't poison himself." He walked over to Cathy and took off the duct tape. "Care to fill in the blanks?"

Her tear-filled eyes turned to rage as she looked

242 KARI LEE TOWNSEND

beyond him. "Why don't you ask Cole's brother-in-law."

We all turned around to find Miles holding a 9-millimeter gun on us.

"Miles?" Cole sputtered.

"*Ex*-brother-in-law," Miles ground out. "Zack didn't kill Gunther. I did."

I sucked in a breath. That's why my nails had dug into Cole's arm over his Three-Musketeer tattoo. And Miles had said over and over not to worry, that justice would prevail. I'd had no idea he'd been talking about wanting justice himself.

"You? Why?" Cole sounded broken.

"You killed my sister," Miles sneered, looking deranged. "She'll never have babies. She was my only sibling. My best friend." His voice hitched. "Your new wife's babies should be hers. They should be my nieces or nephews."

"Why not just kill me and be done with it?" Cole said devastated.

"I wanted you to suffer for years like I have." The pain in Miles' eyes was burning bright, making him irrational. "I wanted you behind bars, missing out on your babies growing up and losing your wife like I lost my sister."

"Then why did I see Zack steal the gun and Cathy hide it?" I asked, confused. My visions always came true, but sometimes it took a bit to understand what they meant.

"Miles was Zack's supplier. He had him right where he wanted him. Zack was so afraid Miles would cut him off, that he would do whatever he wanted," Cathy said. "I'm so sorry, Cole. I had to help him, but neither one of us could live with ourselves. Zack was going to come forward at the chili festival, but Miles poisoned his bowl when he was *helping* Jo out. I visited Zack in the hospital, and he begged me to return Cole's gun to clear his name. Zack knew he was going to stay in the hospital to detox once and for all so he could finally be free of Miles, but Miles figured it out and kidnapped me to draw you all here."

"That's right. You and Zack ruined my plans. You're traitors. Now you all have to pay." Miles lifted his gun. "A dead Cole is better than nothing."

"You can't shoot in every direction at once, Miles," Mitch said, his eyes locking with Cole's briefly then settling back onto Miles. "One of us will get to you before you're done. You won't make it out of here alive."

"I don't care if I die." He moved his gun to Cole. "So long as he dies first."

Sirens wailed off in the distance. Miles turned his head toward the window, looking startled. Cole took two steps and dove. Miles turned back, his eyes wide and crazy as he pulled the trigger. Cole hit the underside of his arm at the last second and the bullet lodged into the wooden roof of the cabin. Cole flattened Miles to the floor with a tight grip on the wrist of the hand which still held the gun. Cole balled his free hand into a fist, landing a right hook to Miles' jaw. He pulled back for another swing but the burning anger in his eyes faded to sorrow as he stared down at Miles, both men breathing hard.

"You're my brother, man," Cole whispered, and hung his head. "Why can't you see I loved her too? So very much." He sniffed back the memory, shaking his head. "A part of me died when I lost her. I lost myself to that darkness, man. I didn't care what happened. And then I found Jo. There will never be another Faith. But Jo has believed in me and showed me I'm capable of loving and being loved. She's making me a

KARI LEE TOWNSEND

father." He leaned closer to Miles' face and we all stood in silence watching it play out, moved by Cole's truthful confession. "The only one who would have suffered from your actions are those three innocent people. But you never thought of that, did you? Faith would be so disappointed."

A brief moment of regret flashed across Miles' face before he looked away, unable to speak.

Mitch sprang into action, securing Miles' gun and putting the cuffs on him. He pulled Cole off of him and squeezed his shoulder. "It's over, buddy. It's finally over."

EPILOGUE

Two weeks later, Winterfest was over, and life went on.

All the murders had been solved, the tourists had moved on, and life was back to normal. Miles was arrested and deemed mentally ill. He was finally getting the help he needed, which Cole was happy about. No matter what Miles had done, Cole had forgiven him, saying he would still always be his brother. And Jo supported Cole in any decision he made, no matter what.

Zack was fully detoxed and released from the hospital. Cole refused to press charges over Zack stealing his gun and Cathy hiding it. He was glad Zack had found a way to get off drugs, and he understood why Cathy did what she did. Cole would do anything to help his family. Cathy understood that Cole couldn't have her work for him anymore. She and Zack decided to leave Divinity for a fresh start together this time.

The inn was fully open and operational, and I had decided having my parents around wasn't so bad after all. Family. That was what life was all about. After nearly losing my own life, I had reflected on what was most important to me. Even if I never had children, I still had a family, and Mitch was the biggest part of that.

We sat by the fire in our living room, staring at the flames, comfortable in the silence between us. I think we were both just happy to be together. It was finally time to have that talk we'd both been putting off for so long, but I wasn't afraid anymore. I knew no matter what, I wanted a future with Mitch.

"Mitch, I—"

"Sunny, I—"

We spoke at the same time and laughed.

"Ladies first," he said, but I never got the chance to speak.

The phone rang.

I bit my lip, trying to ignore it, but couldn't stop bouncing in my seat barely able to sit still.

Mitch smiled softly. "Go ahead. Answer it. You know you want to."

"Really? Are you sure?"

"Yes. Everything else can wait."

"I love you!" I kissed him soundly on the mouth, then bolted to the phone on the table. "Hello?" I paced back and forth, grinning like an idiot, but I couldn't help myself. "Oh, that's so amazing, Cole. I'm so excited for you both." My gaze met Mitch's, and he nodded without me even having to ask the question. "Yes, we'll be right there."

Ten minutes later, we pulled up to Divinity Hospital. The car wasn't even parked before I bolted out the door. For once my big detective with twice my stride had to hurry to keep up with me. We checked in at the front desk then made our way to the maternity ward, where we met Jo and Cole outside the nursery room window. Like most twins, they were born early and being observed, but Cole had said they were healthy and bigger than most.

I expected no less from the sasquatch.

I took one look through the window and my heart burst into a million pieces. Two beautiful blue bassinets were side-by-side, right in front. The babies were identical and the spitting image of Cole, with their mama's fiery red hair and spirit, based on the squalling going on. Nothing had ever sounded better to me. I wrapped my arms around Jo and gave her the biggest hug, while Mitch shook Cole's hand.

Tears were running down both our faces when I pulled back to look my best friend in the eyes. "You did it, Mama."

"I did, didn't I?" She had love written all over her face.

"You look great," I added.

"I feel like I've been run over by two tanks, but I'm so happy."

"Congrats, man." Mitch clapped Cole on the shoulder.

Cole beamed as he handed him a cigar, and Mitch put it in his pocket for later. "We have something we want to ask you guys," Cole said.

"Ask away." I smiled. "We'd do anything for you guys. I hope you know that by now."

Cole looked at Jo. "You do the honors, honey."

"We want you two to be the godparents of the twins," Jo's voice cracked when she spoke, filled with emotion. "We can't think of anyone who would do a better job of raising our boys if anything were to ever happen to us."

"Yes," I said without hesitation, knowing this was probably as close as I would ever get to being a mother. My heart was achingly full.

"Of course," Mitch said a moment later, looking terrified.

We didn't say anything more about that as we all went back to Jo's room and stayed for a while to visit. When she began to tire, we took our leave. We had just climbed into Mitch's truck, when I turned to him and said, "May first."

"What about May first?" He looked confused as he started the truck, turning on the heat and putting the truck in gear.

"That's our wedding date."

He paused for a moment, staring straight ahead, and then he put the truck back in park. He looked me in the eye. "You picked a wedding date?"

"Yes."

"Just like that?"

I nodded. "Just like that."

"Without checking your horoscope charts?"

"No need."

"Why?" He looked skeptical.

"I would marry you on any day at any time. I've realized there are things in my life I can live without, but there is only one thing I can't live without. And that's you. I love you more than life itself, Mitchel Stone. So, Grumpy Pants, will you marry me on May first?"

He traced every inch of my face with his adoring gaze before he answered. "On one condition, Sunshine Meadows."

"What's that?"

"You agree to have my babies, Tink."

Tears sprang to my eyes, and my heart cracked wide open at the lengths this man would go to for me to be happy. "Mitch, you don't have to do that."

"Actually, I do." He brushed away my tears with his thumb. "You see when I thought I lost you, I realized something, too. I don't want to miss out on any part of you. I might be scared to death, and overprotective, and drive you nuts as a father," he inhaled a deep breath, "but I can promise I will always be there and try my best."

"So, is that a yes?" I asked.

"Yes, Tink, I would love nothing more than to make you my wife."

I threw myself across the console until I landed in his lap and kissed his whole face.

"What are you doing?" he said on a chuckle between kisses.

I pulled away just enough to respond, "Working on that condition." Then I kissed him with every bit of love in my heart, not needing a horoscope to know our future looked brighter than ever.

ABOUT THE AUTHOR

Kari Lee Townsend is a National Bestselling Author of mysteries & a tween superhero series. She also writes romance and women's fiction as Kari Lee Harmon. With a background in English education, she's now a full-time writer, wife to her own superhero, mom of 3 sons, 1 darling diva, 1 daughter-in-law & 2 lovable fur babies. These days you'll find her walking her dogs or hard at work on her next story, living a blessed life.

OTHER BOOKS BY KARI LEE HARMON